BLOOM

BLOOM (*noun*) Date: 13th century
1 a : flower **b :** the flowering state **c :** a period of flowering
2 a : a state or time of beauty, freshness, and vigor
b : a state or time of high development or achievement

BLOOM

Queer Fiction, Art, Poetry & More

VOLUME I, ISSUE 2

SUMMER 2004

BLOOM

P.O. BOX 1231
OLD CHELSEA STATION
NEW YORK, NY 10011

BLOOM is published twice a year by Arts in Bloom Project, Inc., a non-profit dedicated to queer artists, writers, and audiences. Tax-deductible donations may be made to BLOOM through our fiscal sponsor, Astraea, Inc. For more information, please contact Charles Flowers at info@bloommagazine.org or at (646) 239-9790.

EDITORIAL POLICY

BLOOM does not discriminate against the imagination. Gardeners must identify as Queer (LGBT), but the flora of their labor need not serve any pre-conceived notion of beauty. Peonies, sweet williams, ragweed, and gladiolas—every shade & shape of blossom—are all welcome. Let the garden grow.

SUBMISSION POLICY

BLOOM publishes poetry, fiction, memoir, essay, travelogue, and any other piece of writing that dazzles us. We are also pleased to present artwork that offers a fresh, sexy, startling, and/or original view of the world. Poetry: Send 3-5 poems, no more than 10 pages. Prose: Send manuscripts of 25 or fewer pages—double-spaced, of course. Art: Send a disk or slides. With all submissions, please include a SASE if you would like us to return your materials. We do not accept electronic submissions.

VISIT

www.bloommagazine.org
for more information.

ISSN 1550-3291

In Memoriam
Thom Gunn
(1929-2004)

BLOOM

would like to acknowledge the following donors

FOUNDERS OF BLOOM

Robert Jaquay
Mitchell Waters

FRIENDS OF BLOOM

John Ashbery
John Elliott

CONTENTS

FICTION

JOHN WEIR
How to Disappear Completely   I

E. J. LEVY
My Life in Theory   27

MARY BETH CASCHETTA
Hands of God   109

JOHN ROWELL
Elementary Education   127

MICHELLE CLIFF
Crocodilopolis   161

ESSAY

CLIFFORD CHASE
The Tooth Fairy   71

ART

ROXA SMITH
Renaissance Mindscape   55

TIM DOUD
Portraits   63

INTERVIEW

CHRISTOPHER HENNESSY
Breaking Past the Margins,
an interview with D. A. Powell   89

POETRY

REGINALD HARRIS
The Ring Walk   16

ANGELIQUE CHAMBERS
Driving   17
Bottom Space—A Negotiation   19

RAFAEL CAMPO
Personal Mythology   22

DAVID GROFF
Milton   23

MENDI LEWIS OBADIKE
Strut   25

ELAINE SEXTON
To Summer   45

DANIEL HALL
At the Nursery   46

MARY ANN McFADDEN
Roosters   47
San Ignacio Lagoon, Clear Water   49

TIMOTHY LIU
The Crisis   51
The Marriage   52

CARL PHILLIPS
Shadow-Land   53

D. A POWELL
[dogs and boys can treat you like trash.
and dogs do love trash]   105

[when you touch down upon this earth.
little reindeers]   106

CHRISTOPHER HENNESSY
Sick Room   107

MARILYN HACKER
Glose   121

SUZANNE GARDINIER
Dialogue 21/The reunion   123
Dialogue 55/To be continued   124

HOLLY IGLESIAS
Conceptual Art   125

CHERYL B.
Reasons to Stop   151

LETTA NEELY
miscellaneous Rifts on Friction
(meant to acknowledge some)   153

CARL MORSE
On a Christmas Card that Came Back
Stamped "Deceased"   155

QWO-LI DRISKILL
Gay Nigger Number One   158

RON MOHRING
The Sound   172

GRETCHEN PRIMACK
Space Exploration   174

STACEY WAITE
On the Occasion of Being Mistaken for a Boy
by the Umpire in the Little League
Conference Championship   177

TIFFANY LYNN WONG
Ketchup and French Fries   178

DEAN KOSTOS
Magus   179

GAIL HANLON
Hummingbird   182

CONTRIBUTORS   183

"In this place, I'm the 'other,' which means I'm from Manhattan; I don't have foreskin; I don't speak Spanish, or Russian, or Korean; I don't have children or a wife; I live alone; I'm unbaptized; I don't pray to God. Plus, unlike them, I'm, you know, 'gay.'"

JOHN WEIR

How to Disappear Completely

Y OU SHOULD SEE the embarrassing poems I've written about him. Andy: a straight guy half my age. My former student. Lives with his mom. What was I thinking? After school, when I've been teaching late and reading student work, I walk from the Queens College campus to Forest Hills, two miles through the center of Queens to the Manhattan-bound F train at Queens Boulevard. The MTA is a traveling frat house past midnight, just the dudes slumped in their seats or tuned into headphones, holding Discmen delicately in their laps. In the early morning I go home with other men and scribble poems in the backs of books.

It's all I've written for months, these odes to him. I scrawled one on the flyleaf of a book by Vladimir Mayakovsky. Did I figure I was nineteen? "I Feel My 'I' Is Much Too Small for Me," the poem is called, a quote from Mayakovsky's "Cloud in Trousers."

I wrote another on the last page of Roland Barthes's *The Pleasure of the Text*. Yes, I'm pretentious. Plus, I'm teaching a course in post-modernism. It wasn't my idea. The students asked for it. They heard a rumor I was intertextual, and maybe it's true: I scribble poetry on Barthes.

"Cruising" is the name of the poem. "I'm on a concrete slab in front of Burger King," it starts, and then I want to tell you the time: 2:26 p.m., March 20, the last day before the first of spring, the year 2001. "I'm in East Elmhurst, Queens, New York, Astoria Boulevard, right below the flight path of La Guardia Airport."

It's Tuesday afternoon, and the sun is burning off the winter chill. Yo-dudes drive by in SUVs pumping rap, their windows unrolled. Tractor trailers shift gears, blow smoke. "It's Good for You," a truck advertises. Across the street, which goes both ways, east-west, the Cozy Cabin promises "Show Girls Daily," its windows masked with cardboard. Uphill from the Cozy Cabin is the *Salon del Reino* or the Kingdom Hall of Jehovah's Witnesses.

God is watching, which is too bad, because I've been at the Fair, a pornographic movie theater. It's at Ninety-first Street, lurching over half a block along Astoria Boulevard. Once a movie palace, now it's a Giuliani-era smut house. That is, they show kung fu movies in front to hoodwink the Vice Squad, but in back past the bathrooms are three large viewing rooms screening porn. There's a room for girl-boy sex, a room for boy-boy sex, and a room for interracial sex and chicks with dicks. Girl-girl sex happens in the girl-boy room and in the trannie room. Boy-boy sex is carefully confined, taking place on just one screen, quarantined as if to protect not just others, but itself.

It's the only sexual kick that's uncorrupted by alternatives. Every other brand of porn is polymorphously perverse. Sure, you'll never see two men kissing in a straight porn film. But at least the girls get it on. And there are group gropes in hetero porn where straight men watch each other. Gay guy porn, however, is almost fascistically pure. There's no mixing of perversions: two guys, or five guys, or ten guys fuck. It's humorless and male. No pleasure outside of the penis. No pain, either.

I'm gay because I hate not women, but men. I'm terrified of men, which means, of course, that I can't resist them. I'm dying to know how it feels to be a man. I don't want to touch them, I want to become them. Him. Andy's back. If I could press my face to his back, I'm sure I'd be ready for God—for punishment or mercy. I want to be inside him, to know how it feels to swing from that center. Held in by his muscles, pinned and secure. His back, the small of his back. "My ass," he said once, ruefully, meaning, "All my weight's in my ass." It was affectionate and sorry. I want him to talk about me like that. Is that gay? I don't want to be gay. Gay guys are different from men, and I want to be the same as men, which is what "homosexual" means: "resemblance" not "desire." I yearn for what I'm not.

I'm not Andy. I'm an untenured college professor in a dirty movie theater that runs kung fu films to placate the police. They're shown in the front of the house before a vast empty orchestra and a grand balcony that is permanently closed. Men linger smoking in the orchestra's foyer, lounging on puffy couches and chairs. You can sit and chat, or play video games, or stand against the chin-high oak divider behind the last row of auditorium seats, your head in your hands or your arms at your sides, waiting for the fifty-year-old Irish firefighter in work boots and a Mets cap to sidle up to you and let a polite and silent interval pass before he puts his hand on your ass.

The neighborhood is half black and half Latino, so the Fair is crowded with black men with shaved heads or smooth conks or dread locks, wearing sweat suits and business suits; and there are men from Argentina, Mexico, Brazil, Peru, Colombia, Ecuador, El Salvador, and the Dominican Republic. Married dudes from Merrick, Long Island, stop by on their way home from work. They're Irish, German, Italian, Greek, and Jewish, carrying attaché cases and wearing gold chains and gold rings.

The age range is forty to sixty. If young guys show up, they're often Vietnamese or Taiwanese or Malaysian. No one looks like me: doughy WASPy white guy dressed like a preppie in khakis and a Brooks Brothers shirt. In this place, I'm the "other," which means I'm from Manhattan; I don't have foreskin; I don't speak Spanish, or Russian, or Korean; I don't have children or a wife; I live alone; I'm unbaptized; I don't pray to God. Plus, unlike them, I'm, you know, "gay." Most of the men at the Fair would say they are straight. That's the story of my life since high school. Even in a homo jerk-off parlor, I'm the only fag around.

In any case, everybody plays it straight. Here's the game: You hang in the boy-girl porno room for an hour, lounging in the low-slung leatherette reclining seats or standing against the wall, smoking butts and talking with your buddies. Then you wander, just wander, first to the john, then across the hall and quickly as possible through the boy-boy room. You might linger in the trannie room for a minute, as if you were an anthropologist reading fragments of Icelandic runes. Finally, you turn casually and head to the video "buddy" booths in back, which line two long hallways. Each booth is the size of a jani-tor's closet in a New York City public school.

There are about ten booths along each hall. Today I shared one with my "buddy" Rico. I think that's what he said his name was, though it might have been "Ricky," or "Rocky," or "Rocco." We did-n't have a language in common. I asked his birthday and he pointed at his watch. "Where do you live?" I said, and again he laid his index finger obscurely but definitely on the face of his watch. If I had been able to speak Spanish, he probably wouldn't have wanted to talk, conversation being, duh, not the point of human contact in a stroke parlor. Still, I like to get whatever information I can: name, age, native language, childhood home, astrological sign. Rico seemed to be close to my age, though he might have been fifty. He was wearing a gold band on his left ring finger. I figured he was a Pisces, because he liked to kiss.

If he wasn't my first choice, he also wasn't my last. The whole thing was an accident, really: my being in East Elmhurst at such an hour on such a day. When I left Manhattan this afternoon, I was headed for school. I was due to teach my evening class in postmod-ernism, where we were going to discuss Barthes's notions of "pleas-ure" and "bliss." I ended up at a porno movie theater because I got on the wrong train and fell in love with a couple.

They were Russian, and it was the Number 7. I meant to be on the R. I was buying lunch at Dean and De Luca's on Broadway near

Houston Street, and there was an N/R station next door. My face buried in Barthes, I mistakenly got on the N. After crossing under the East River, the train rose above ground, which the R doesn't do. As soon as I saw daylight, I knew I was way off track. The N would take me to jail, not college: it ends a bus ride away from Riker's Island. So I switched for the local to Flushing, where I could get a bus to campus.

Except that I was hijacked by a guy on the Number 7 holding his girlfriend's hand. They were speaking Russian, which is odd, because Russian immigrants in Queens mostly live along the G or E or F or R, in Forest Hills or Lefrak City. So these two people were out of place. He had a widow's peak, and she was wearing wraparound sunglasses like Yoko Ono. She was small and fine and he was lanky and wired and stroking her hand. I watched him stroking and stroking her thumb with his hand. He held her fingers laced through his, and he rubbed her thumb with the side of his index finger.

What's the connection that happens between strangers on a train? I'm watching them, they're not aware of me. But they're causing the fuzz at the back of my head and the tight feeling in my stomach. It's like Ernest Hemingway watching a fish. Occupational hazard: As an English teacher, I quote Hemingway, or rather, Nick Adams in "The Big Two-Hearted River," arriving by train at a burned-out town, walking past acres of scorched timber, everything charred and ash—even the grasshoppers' bellies are black—to a bridge across a river. Seeing the water, he thinks, Well, at least the river is there. And in the river are fish, and they are arching out of the water and turning and moving their fins and slicing back into the current; and watching them, in his watching and in their being watched, Nick feels "all the old feeling."

He feels something watching a fish. Of course, the fish doesn't know, or care, about Nick's feelings. The fish is unconscious, oblivious to Nick. And just as Nick and maybe Hemingway take pleasure in looking without being noticed or known, so do I. Watching the couple on the train, my head is cottony and my belly is tight. I'm wondering how it's possible to, whatever, flush red, feel something, have a whole relationship with someone who isn't aware you exist. I'm hooked on people who don't see me. We're tied together, though

I'm the only one who senses the taut line from my gut to her finger, his hand. The way he touches and squeezes and caresses her thumb is scary and exciting. It's too much, he won't leave her alone, he leans over her and grabs her free hand and doesn't let go. If I were her, I'd ask him to stop. But I don't want him to stop.

When they get off the train at Elmhurst Avenue and Ninetieth Street, six stations ahead of mine, I'm pulled out after them by the strength of the connection they don't see or suspect. My following them feels involuntary, which is not to say I don't know it's invasive: I'm a grown man on my way to teach a roomful of graduate students about "pleasure" and "bliss," and I have turned, halfway there, into a stalker, a stealthy Hemingway quoter, a creep.

Out on the train platform, she goes on ahead, and for a minute I think they've separated, because he's suddenly alone. His hair is sandy brown and thinning in front and I don't think he buys his own clothes. The sheer shirt and the pants—white painter's pants tight at the waist—seem like her choice. He's got a brown mole on his right cheek, thick blunt fingers, wide shoulders, and a funny walk. He nearly skips after her when he finds her down on the street. There she is, ahead of him, and he races to reach her, putting his arms around her shoulders and neck from the back.

I know I'm being perverse. I want to call the police on myself. So I lose them, walking to Ninety-second Street and turning north, heading up through Jackson Heights to East Elmhurst, "accidentally" reaching the Fair.

You never "decide" to go into a porno house. Anyway, I don't. It's not like planning a trip to the mall. Suddenly, I'm here. "Oh, look, gay porn, who knew?" Of course, I walked here directly, if leisurely, all the while telling myself that it's a pleasant day to stroll through the neighborhoods of Queens. Forget that I've got class to teach in two hours. Until the last half-block, when I make a deliberate turn into the entryway of the movie theater, I'm convinced I have other plans. I'll stop at a pay phone, call Andy, pray his mom doesn't answer. "Yo, dude. I'm in East Elmhurst, which, to get here from Elmhurst, you have to walk *north*. Figure that." Then I'll snag a cab on Astoria Boulevard and reach school way before class.

Of course, there are no yellow cabs cruising East Elmhurst. And the route to Queens College, by way of surface roads, is blocked at almost every turn by huge highways. A cab would have to spin me a long way out of the way in order to come back a short distance correctly. You see my dilemma. Why not go jerk off? I pass through the theater's gaping entryway, under the giant marquee—"FIRST RUN IN QUEENS," it says, coyly, as if you could walk inside and catch the new hit with Ed Norton—pay my dough to the Indian man behind the ticket booth, spin through the turnstile, and enter the Fair.

Like all the guys, I start in the boy-girl room. But I can't watch porn for long. It wouldn't matter if Omar Epps were doing Benicio del Toro, or Drew Barrymore were smooching Halle Berry. Porno makes everything look like a training film for garage mechanics: in, out, shaft, piston. Is that all there is?

After a minute, I cross the hall, through the boy-boy room, past chicks with dicks, to the buddy booths. Lining the halls are maybe twenty guys, potential "buddies," mostly in their fifties, their faces creased as sharecroppers' in a photo essay by Walker Evans. Men with big hands and chipped nails, men with their hair combed carefully in place, men in blue jeans and parkas, plain men. I think of immigrants to New York in the early 1900s, when guys on their own in lower Manhattan got tired of putting off sex until the day they had money enough to send home for their girlfriends and wives. So they went to a huge beer house on the Bowery, where boys gowned like Gibson girls served drinks and then had sex for pay in rooms upstairs.

That makes public sex between men sound quaint and historic. But I'd be lying if I didn't admit that the Fair is depressing. With men, there's always a game, and the winner of every porno palace is the guy who gets to reject the most people. The victor today is an Italian guy who looks like a stand-in for Robert De Niro in *The Godfather II*. He's strutting, angular, groomed, compact, well-dressed, quick-moving, all business. If you glance at him, he frowns. Lighting cigarettes, checking his watch, he has convinced himself that he's at a board meeting closing a deal, or scouting leftie pitchers. Anything but prowling the oiled halls of a crumbling smut house for a guy who'll put a finger up his butt.

Here is how I know I'm not a man: Men are people who can stand completely grim and immobile for hours dreaming of sex. In strip parlors, they lounge at the lip of the stage not moving, while someone gorgeous squats naked above them, legs spread. Slumped in chairs in porno theaters, they sit inert as rutabaga bulbs watching naked people flash exquisite body parts across the screen. In the hallways of the Fair, guys stand still as if mounted on corkboard, maybe not even alive. Pornographic sex is obviously a sedative. It doesn't excite, it deflates. The problem with American youth is that they don't watch *enough* pornography. Mothers, if you want your children docile and depressed, send them to the smut house.

In other words, I'm walking around and no one is checking me out. Half an hour's gone. I'm running out of time. I paid $8.50 at the door, I want my money's worth of joy. Which is when Rico turns up. I'm circling the halls for the seventeenth time, and he's in the corner, next to the fire door, and he looks at me. No smile, nothing that nice. Just a glance, our eyes meet, and that's my signal. Is he attractive? Sure, everyone's attractive. Especially when you're running out of time. I'm a fatalist with sex: If you happen to want me, I'm yours. Which sometimes gets me in trouble. Not here, of course, if "trouble" means falling in love. You don't fall in love in video booths, except for ten minutes, and I've got twenty. Rico steps into a booth and I follow.

So here I am, an English teacher still unable to define "bliss" but standing with Rico in a booth as big as a bathroom stall. There's a tiny TV screen near the door showing four channels of porn: guy-in-leather, guy-in-gym-shorts, girl-with-tongue-stud. The other channel is static. Sometimes men who go with you into a booth will watch the screen, not you, while you both jerk off. Rico puts his arms around me, hugs me, kisses my neck. I'm leaning against the wall. A knee-high bench is built into the wall, and I take off my coat and put it on the bench with my knapsack.

Inside my knapsack is a $7.00 tuna fish sandwich that I bought at Dean and De Luca's, thinking, "I'll save this for later." I didn't want to eat on the train, because I was lost in *The Pleasure of the Text*. Barthes kept talking about "hermeneutics," which is Greek for "interpretation," though it also kind of means money: it's from a root word for "assigning values to things you exchange." Rico has got his hand in my pants. He is rubbing my penis through my boxer shorts, which I bought at the K-Mart on Astor Place after Andy told me that he got all his underwear at "the pharmacy."

"What pharmacy?'" I said.

"Any pharmacy," he told me.

Then Andy lifted his shirt and showed me his shorts, which, like all men in America under the age of twenty-eight, he wears above the waist of his jeans. There was the sudden aching gap of skin between his shirt and shorts. "Is not the most erotic portion of the body *where the garment gapes?*" Barthes asks, in *The Pleasure of the Text*, his words jutting into italics. Whenever you see "skin flashing between two articles of clothing," he says, "it is this flash itself which seduces." And quickly disappears, which is the true joy: knowing joy will end. In other words, bliss is loss. Desire is whatever you're losing.

"You'll lose money buying them anywhere else," Andy said, and he was right. K-Mart was selling three pairs of boxer shorts for $9.95, way cheaper than the Gap. I bought nine pairs. The pair that Rico is rubbing his flat palm against is white with red pencil stripes.

Then he undoes my zipper.

Suddenly there's a dead guy in the room with me. Not Rico, but my best friend Dave, who died of AIDS in 1994. I'm Norman Mailer: mention sex, I'm instantly thinking of death. Is that "sex-negative?" Whatever, I'm a gay man who has lived in New York for twenty-one years—for these *past* twenty-one years—and I have watched a lot of people die. Everything reminds me of death. Why should sex be an exception? Dave died just a few months before all the new life-saving drugs became available. He was a mean bastard while he was dying, but up until the last few months of his life, he was delightfully silly. Mention sex to David, and he came up not with death but with a party game: "In the movie of your life, who would play your penis?"

"Who is your penis?" Dave asks from the grave, which, considering that I've got Rico's hand in my pants, is kind of wrecking the moment. Placating Dave, I say, "Angela Bassett."

"That's cheating," Dave says.

"All right," I say. "Eric Stoltz."

"Eric *Stoltz*?"

"You know, sturdy, pink, supportive. Not the lead but often an intriguing cameo. Better for television, really: small-screen, German-Irish, completely functional, thank you very much, and secretly capable of wacky outbursts. *Stoltz* means 'pride' in German," I add, modestly.

That silences David. He's gone. The dead want to name my dick, but Rico, the living, is holding it, pulling it out of my pants. Now I'm a fully dressed man in a booth talking silently with a ghost while a stranger in jeans and a T-shirt gets my penis out in the open, poking naked through my shorts and zipper.

And he tentatively touches it. Which completely banishes David, thank God. I'm alive, and I won't lie: There's the wonderful encompassing shock of a guy putting his hand all the way around your penis.

"What's your name?" I ask him, because if you touch my penis, I'm in love with you, and I want to hear him speak, this object of my love. I ask again, "What's your name?" He's just my height, his hair is fine and brown. He leans back and pulls off his shirt, and there's a cross on a chain hanging on his chest, and I'm thinking, "Jesus hung out with tax collectors, who is He to judge?"

There isn't much hair on his chest. He's thick-chested. His belly is big but solid. He undoes my pants and pulls my trousers and shorts to my knees, and then he raises my T-shirt and shirt and sweater—I'm wearing a powder blue sweater vest, which, my students say, makes me look Republican—and kisses my nipple, the left one, over my heart.

Well, he's holding me. My trousers and shorts are at my ankles. "What," I ask him, closing my eyes, putting my arms around his back, wondering if I should take off my watch, which is big and blocky with the face on the inside, against my inner wrist. I'm scraping my watch across his back as I stroke his shoulders. But if I take it off, I'll forget it. So I harrow his back. His head is under my T-shirt and shirt and sweater vest. "What," I repeat, "is your name?"

Our video screen is tuned to boy-in-leather, who's saying, "Faggot, suck my dick."

I never understand the preferred conceit of gay male porn, which is that somebody has to not want it. There's one guy who's straight and won't do it, and a faggot who constantly does. Though I guess that's me and everyone I've ever loved. On the other hand, Rico kisses me. He comes out from under my shirts and kisses me on the lips. He kisses me quick, once, twice, wraps himself entirely around me, holds me as tight as he can, kisses me again. We're kissing for real, now, and I'm thinking, Well, I hope he doesn't have herpes. Then I remember that there are other things I don't yet know about him: his name, and whether he has a functioning penis.

I undo his fly, unsnap his trousers, unbuckle his belt, and push down his pants. He's wearing pink bikini underwear, which means for certain that he doesn't speak English. He pulls his underwear down, and I say again, holding his penis—I take it in my hand not greedily or expectantly, or as if it were ever my right, but with an air of what Tennessee Williams would call "tender protection," I guess I *am* a fag, I can't touch a strange man's penis without quoting Tennessee Williams—I ask him again, "What's your name?" And that's when he tells me, with his dick in my hand. "Rico," he says, or "Ricky," or, "Rocco," or, "Rocky," or "Enrique," or maybe he mis-understood, maybe he was answering another question that I didn't think I'd asked.

So now we're two guys naked to the ankles. Or, rather, he's naked, I'm not. So I get shirtless, too. I think sides are supposed to be even. I drop my shirts and sweater to the bench with my knapsack and coat, and we're both nude with our pants and shorts around our feet. He's sucking my nipples again.

"That's right, faggot," says the guy on the video, which is, like, flashback to high school. I hit the channel button and change to static.

Rico and I kiss for a long time. Our skin pressed together, shoulder to thigh, we kiss. He won't talk but he likes to kiss. My watch has a button that lets you light its face to see the time, and I press it: still an hour before school. I lean back. He's jerking me off. I hold his penis. He has lumpy testicles held up close to his flesh and his penis is shaped like him, blunt and big-headed, but, unlike him, oddly aloof. He's sucking my nipples like I have taken my only son in my arms and nursed him, my hand on the back of his head, saying, "Rico," over and over, "Rico," softly, and he doesn't make a sound, he's sucking my nipples. His penis is Willem Dafoe. It's part of the action but it doesn't belong in this film. It should be in a French film, not this sloppy human American thing in which a grown man suckles another full-grown man with pink bikini underwear tangling in his shoelaces. And suddenly Rico yells, or, really, cries, and he comes on my thighs, and all over my discount K-Mart boxer shorts that Andy got me to buy.

He comes and I don't. I smile apologetically. It's an unwritten smut house rule that you both come at once, so your buddy doesn't have to get you off when he's already splattered. But Rico smiles wistfully, and then, kindly and patiently, he holds me with his arm around my shoulders and his head pressed to my neck while he jerks me off. He's watching, we're both watching me. Because in the second before I come—more smut house etiquette—I have to turn sharply away so that I blast, not on us, or on the bench where my bag is packed with lunch and Roland Barthes, but against the wall and on the floor, so no one gets slimed or soaked.

I'm done, we don't speak. He dresses quickly, but he waits while I clean up, which takes awhile, because my shorts are shot. They're wet with him. I have to remove my shoes, my trousers and shorts, wad Andy's boxers, wipe myself with them, and drop them on the bench, leaving them behind.

He watches and waits. When I'm dressed, he grins, hugs me, turns to go, reaches out, puts his hand on my face, his palm and fingers on my cheek—"Every narrative," Barthes says, "is a staging of the absent father"—and he touches my face. "Later, man," I tell him. He goes out the door, I close it, wait a second, lean against the wall, close my eyes, remember, remember his hand.

Because joy, for me, isn't just sex. Sure, I liked his touching my dick. But it would have been okay if he wanted something else, if he asked to be dandled or paddled or tweaked. There was a guy once who called me his queer buddy and told me to tie his work boots to his testicles. "Whatever, man," I said. I don't mind what anyone wants. The payoff, for me, the value-exchange, is in the moment afterwards, when we're dressed again as men, and he can't speak English, and I don't speak anything else, and he hugs me, and it's like, "Yo, man, I'm so alone."

There's my joy, how men are lonely.

I'm in love with male loneliness.

Women are supposed to be lonely. I watched those movies when I was growing up in the '60s and '70s, every afternoon on Channel 7, 1940s Warner Brothers movies full of powerful women feeling painfully incomplete without a man—which, they would obviously never need a man in the actual world. What could Bette Davis or Joan Crawford want from a man? I will never be as self-sufficient as those women. But the fiction was they were lonely, and their loneliness was dramatic, often histrionic, even hysterical, and they said they were nothing without men.

At the time, I believed them. I even grew up thinking I would be like them, a lonely woman missing men. Freud says we're all born little boys and only girls have to become something else, but that's not right, I'm sure I was a girl. And the difference between men and me is that I became a lonely woman and they grew into lonely men.

Now I want to be what men are, helplessly lonely. It's men who need other men. Can I have that moment with you? Can I have that masculine distance, disappearance, vanishing, absence, remove, aloofness, withdrawal, that silent moment after sex with someone whose name I don't know who sucked my nipples, held my penis, cried like a child and spilled himself across my thighs? He was helpless in that instant. The best thing about sex is helplessness, the stuff you can't do. He couldn't not come. I mean, for a minute, he had to be in the room, with me. And afterwards, he put his hand on my face and said, "Bye." In whatever language. And I said, "Good-bye."

Outside, on Astoria Boulevard, there's no cab, of course. I've got time. I sit in front of Burger King and eat my sandwich from Dean and DeLuca's.

When I'm done, I walk along Astoria Boulevard to the Van Wyck Expressway, taking the beautiful curve of the entrance ramp up into traffic. I'm a grown man fully dressed walking along an expressway. It's spring, cars honk, not happily; people think I'm an idiot. Getting off the highway, I climb over concrete dividers, cut through traffic on entrance and exit ramps, reach grass, come to the big empty parking lot of Shea Stadium, which is blue. Then I'm on Roosevelt Avenue, on a bridge that goes over the Van Wyck Expressway and under the Flushing Number 7 train. This is where Nick Carraway and Tom Buchanan got off the train to visit Tom's lover Myrtle in Fitzgerald's valley of ashes. It's now a junkyard for wrecked cars, and it smells of sewage and vegetable rot.

Spin around above the waste and you can get a whiff of industrial waste, and a panoramic view of, you know, the postmodern condition. Texts competing for attention, equally insistent. Identity built from contradictory fragments that lead away from your "self" into nothing. I become what I see: the bruise-red cars of the Flushing local sinking underground across rusted switches and tracks. Planet Earth the greying Unisphere. All the parkways and expressways, the bloodlines Robert Moses laid through the bog, curl over and around each other like live bait in a soup can. And a sign across the Flushing River says "Self Storage."

And if I could have talked to Rico I would have said, guy-like, "Man, I love Queens." I love wreckage and disaster, industrial waste. I love looking at this intersection of highways and trains and planes taking off overhead and cars crashed and the river stagnant below and thinking this is all we can do, this is the best we can ever do, we get off the boat from faraway places, slaughter the people living along the banks of the rivers and streams, and build across the new land a redeemer nation of what? Sewage, slop, waste, rot, rusted steel, the gaping awful failure of a century. Face to face with man's capacity for wonder and we make ourselves, in Flushing, a mess.

Not Manhattan's mess. Manhattan is the pores of the face scrubbed clean with astringent. The rest of the body is here, God's blood and guts and soul and wounds and all. I love the failing body, knowing we'll die. I love the clogged river and the deafening airplanes and the Mets, the fucking Mets. Because the other thing I want is to be nothing, I want to be lonely and nothing. Queens is a good place for that. There are lonely men everywhere here waiting to leave you so they can get close at the last minute. That's bliss.

That's when I feel joy, when I want to be "present." David, while he was dying, was forever asking me to be "present." Well, here I am: leaving you, drifting past, hand on your face, reeking of come, headed for nothing, happy with that. It won't take a moment. Andy. Just give me your hand.

REGINALD HARRIS

The Ring Walk

We enter to the roar of voices
pulling themselves apart.
The air has razors in it,
music pumping like a heart in lust
smelling satisfaction straight ahead.
The crowd's a screaming animal
thirsting for blood—
      I'll make sure it's someone else's
                not my own.

A duck under the ropes and quick
dance around the ring inhaling every eye's desire
turns me to steel, the shouting of my name
furious polish on my skin.
      I rule the world—
           one lucky punch away from being nobody.

Final instructions
buzz past my ears, the touch of gloves last
chance to think the other human 'til we're done:
      Now he's just an obstacle, a machine
          of flesh for me to take apart.

The bell
    springs.

We step into a yawning mouth of light
              and life begins.

ANGELIQUE CHAMBERS

Driving

That night it was not safe
to be driving, but we
did anyway—quiet
whirring around in the
pickup cab like snowflakes,
muffling the few sounds we did
make—him tapping his fingers
against the wheel, every so often
saying *can't see shit* to no
one in particular and me shifting
in my seat. And it's not that
I had nothing to say.

I held my hands wide
open, palms up as if
balancing what I was about
to give up in one hand and her
in the other. Snow flew like
a plague of insects, like late night static
TV and I wondered if our
children would have inherited his
cheekbones or grin, if he really would
have bought me the little yellow
house I loved so much and would we
have painted it red? Would I have finally
learned to grow geraniums? And would
his mother have learned to like me
then? Would my mother like me
now?

Would I miss the gravel
and grit of his voice, the

smell of his sweat thick and damp
as new dirt, the press of his penis
and heavy testicles in the small of
my back as I slept? Would I
miss his long hair, the golden fur
of his calves and ass, the scrape of
his beard against my thigh? Could
I really take off the ring, set it on the coffee table
and back away? Could I leave him
behind? And still I said nothing and we
drove on toward home.

Paused at the stop light (the
only one in town) I remembered
last night her hands on
my skin, her hair—cut shorter
and shorter until it bristled
through my fingers, her breasts
damp—tasting like salt and smelling
like bread. She said *I love
you but I won't wait forever.* Her
eyes when I walked down
the hall, her kiss when I ran
back to say goodbye,
again.

When we shuffled into
the house, arms heavy with
packages, noses running
and red I took
off that ring, and
found I had nothing
to say.

Bottom Space—A Negotiation

> "So let me say explicitly, at the risk of sounding foolish, that this is a valentine in its original form, a cunt held open by a woman's trusting fingers."

—Pat Califia, *Macho Sluts*

I'm proud to call myself
a pervert (a title I adopted
after I read somewhere that
real lesbians do not have sex
like *that*). My new motto: I fuck
therefore I am. According to a
high school textbook, endorphins
are the chemicals released
by the brain when an individual eats
chocolate, smokes marijuana, engages
in sexual activity or is in
pain. Fucking is blood
pounding in my ears, sting landing
on top of sweat. To me good
sex will never taste like
vanilla, but according to *The Courage
to Heal*, "for women who are working
to heal beyond their conditioning to
abuse, participating in SM makes
no sense." Survivors hide your
rope. Stop checking out the width
of your date's belt, read politically
correct erotica, practice orgasms
to the tune of *I love you* (Je t'aime
for the exotically inclined).

The Courage to Heal also
tells us that smells are linked to
memories which are linked to bodies
which may explain why the smell of
leather (belts, jackets, boots) makes me
wet. (Being a vegan I've tried to compensate
for this sin. I bought a nylon harness. I sold my
whip, an instrument that could fit every
positive adjective in the English language—sting-y,
sexy, spiffy even—but was leather just the
same.) The smell of leather plays with my
mind the way sound takes you
back the way every time my top hears
a certain song she thinks of her favorite
drag queen, Nikki Fenmore, swaying
hips and swishing tits (bigger than mine but
made of birdseed) on
any given Thursday in Syracuse,
New York. My cunt remembers the
way leather smells smacking
flesh.

Fuck *The Courage to
Heal,* live the life that makes
you burn. Create
drama, reclaim plot. For
example—in this scene the
protagonist (who for the purposes of
this poem shall be known only as a very
naughty girl) has red finger-
nails, holds a whip and can do back
flips in stiletto heels. People, be not
afraid to get on your
knees and breathe in the scent of
leather before sliding off
a boot. Be bad—collect

restraints, watch porn, call
your lover Daddy loud enough to
scare the neighbors. Just say no to
mediocre sex. Transform your
bedroom into the remote alley of your
fantasies. Stop worrying about lubricant
staining your bed sheets. Suck on
something.

Personal Mythology

That's him, the little faggot I remember,
all that hair slicked back with foamy mousse
drying hard as a helmet. There he goes,
his eyes watching his own shape in the mirror,

the outline of his half-hard dick in jeans
and the downy chest hair in the deep V
of his unbuttoned oxford places he
imagines being touched. Dumb kid, he preens

to disco music from the turntable,
some Trojans stolen from his father's stash
soft circles in his wallet with some cash.
He wants to slip towards life through some locked portal,

not knowing what I know now, that his face
will never be more worth seeing. He thinks
he's less like Helen than Achilles, winks
at his jaunty unlit cigarette, blows

a kiss across two decades' emptiness—
how could he have guessed that sex was like pain,
too fleeting a glance at the gods' domain,
the hero's weeping over Patroclus

depicted in his textbook. That damn queer,
I can't forgive his innocence, as if
he might be just like anyone, his love
weak armies crushed in this heart lost to fear.

DAVID GROFF

Milton

Not the poet—though yes,
a poet, aspiring. Old.
At Big Cup he regards us
slickened with testosterone,
his eyes entertained.
Though his full hair helps him
seem a youth in drag
save for the swags of his neck,
he can't but help present
himself as age itself,
a brand of birthmark
we think we won't accrue,
unnerving as June rime
limning a suburban lawn,
as if he were a black man
scouting a Mormon temple.
His melting candle of body,
cupped, burns. He grins.

Compare him to the man-crone
trolling Our Place
in Des Moines with Frank
Fortuna and Dan Grace
two decades ago:
Brutally cruising, drunken,
his halo of hair aflame,
he swaggered to budding men
declaring "You'll be me!,"
his annunciation denunciation,
then stalked off, sated.
The boys, abashed and angry,
decided time was a virus

you just had to swallow.
"The faggot angel of death,"
Frank baptized him.
Now Frank is fifty-one,
commences drinking at noon.

Maybe knowing Frank,
or himself an initiate of crones,
and warhorse of Village cafés
whose soldiers now are wraiths
(who here knows
what old men know?),
Milton acts like he belongs.
He steps among tattoos,
buzzed hair, and bashful mouths,
inhales the caffeine and finds
himself an appropriate chair,
surveying the sipping guys,
while taking care to seem
a clean old man.
He winks, to summon us
to the fallen fruit of himself
that if we've got guts enough
we will pick up and eat.

MENDI LEWIS OBADIKE

Strut

NEW ORLEANS, NIGHT

Our last night in town, my friend is just from her mother
When the elevator catches her made-up face unawares.
Wrapped in myself, I miss the down-turned eyes
But manage to plead, *Come with us,* and she does.

Ours is a party of strangers, as tightly
Bound by lack as by what we hold
Between us. Who knows what could be
Ailing another? Alone as we are,

We make our way through the blacker part
Of the city in a pack. We wear the night
And one another as a perfect skin. This city converts
Our words into whatever magic we need.

We're on the catwalk. This side of Congo Square,
Men buzz, but not to us. Here, they reach
And call to each other as if old friends: *Work,*
Sweetness. This is to the brothers who walk

Among us, who keep aloof but nonetheless, flock
Here. Right now they flank her, my sad friend,
Noting her strut. A few steps behind, I am
Watching them raise the veil of sorrow from her eyes

And send it to the stars. She likes it when they talk
To her in third person: *The girl is fly.* One lifts
Her hand above her head to twirl her. *Hair/shoes,*
Someone whispers. *Skin/hair,* someone whispers back.

"

We liked to tell each other about our little crushes; it kept us on our toes, kept us honest. . . . Our revelations were like a *ménage à trois* without the social awkwardness, and we always made love afterwards with the urgency of adulterers.

"

E. J. LEVY

My Life in Theory

P HILOSOPHERS, IT WOULD SEEM, have little to tell us about love; I know, because I am one. Despite the name *philosopher*—lover of wisdom—we are not known for our success in the realm of Eros. Truth is, our greatest minds have been losers when it came to love. Søren Kierkegaard, for instance, had just one sexual experience in his life and that a failed one, with a prostitute. Perhaps that's because philosophy seeks a system, and love—as any lover knows—is unsystematic in the extreme. Love's a messer-upper, and philosophers, on the whole, are a tidy bunch—at least I am, or was, until we met.

Kate, my girlfriend, introduced us.

I had been away at a regional APA conference, and for most of the flight home, I had been thinking about making love with Kate, the freckled expanse of her skin. So I was disappointed, when I returned home, to find her going on about a new reporter at the paper, recently transferred from one of those N-states in the West— Nebraska or New Mexico. I could tell from the way she spoke of him that she was a little infatuated, but it didn't worry me.

We liked to tell each other about our crushes; it kept us on our toes, kept us honest. We had been together several years by then and shared a belief that we wouldn't stray so long as we kept our theoretical dalliances between us. Our revelations were like a *ménage à trois* without the social awkwardness, and we always made love afterwards with the urgency of adulterers.

Kate and I had met in a Wittgenstein seminar five years before, where she'd impressed us all with her dry wit, long neck, and beautiful breasts. She is not what most people would call a beautiful woman— her expressions are too difficult, too interesting for that—but she is compelling. Though her mother is American, she grew up in South Africa, before her parents' divorce, and the African sun has left its mark—giving her eyes their squint, her mouth its premature lines. She had short copper hair and green eyes and can talk any of us under the table. She dated several of us that term, but I was the only one to last past qualifying exams, and I felt lucky, though luck is not a thing philosophers on the whole take an interest in. Superstition is largely outside our realm of concern. Although we traffic in abstractions, we think ourselves empiricists, skeptics; my peers and I snubbed the mystics among us (the Buberians, as we called them, seemed unrigorous, too sentimental for our taste). We favored Wittgenstein and Nietzsche. We grew up in the eighties, after all.

The night I returned from the APA, as Kate described her new friend, I tried to imagine him, the way one tests a new flavor on the tongue. I tried to see what she saw in him, my interest in him an extension of my interest in her. It was not hard to imagine; she described his face, his voice, his body. "You know the type," she said, with the air of amused and proprietary dismissal that signals a crush, "beauty and the beats—goatee, khakis, the collected work of Bukowski."

I wondered if she wanted to sleep with him. I wondered idly what he'd be like in bed. I'd slept with a few men before, in prep school and as an undergrad; there was something noncommittal in the whole exchange. We were friends, those guys and I; we didn't mistake sex for love. We were after pleasure, biding our time, until we met the right woman and settled down.

IN *PHILOSOPHY MADE SIMPLE*—or PMS, as my students call it—the philosophy textbook from which I'm required to teach at the local university, love gets no mention in the index. *Remorse* does, as do *tyranny* and the *unmover unmoved*. *Rewards* are mentioned, *revenge, respect for others, paradoxes, pain, lying, heat,* and *happiness. Suicide, socialism, abortion,* and *sexual morality.* But *love* is nowhere to be found. To learn about love, evidently, you have to do your own research.

The majority of people seem content to love by rote, to acquiesce to cant—love is true (or untrue), men are dogs, women are nuts, love is hell or makes the world go round. Most do not need to ask what love is, any more than they question what is the good or the real. They live and love and ask questions later. But I couldn't help but wonder, even as I was happy with Kate, *Is this love? In settling down, have we merely settled?*

It occured to me from time to time that the heart might not be the source of my troubles, but the mind. Ever since I'd defended my dissertation in the spring, I'd felt a dull dissatisfaction. The examined life no longer seemed worth living. Kate called it postpartum depression. But I wondered if it might be something more.

My colleagues at the university were little comfort. In the grim warren of grad offices my fellow adjuncts assembled like an accusation. This—they seemed to say—is what education leads to. This is the image of the examined life: frail women in cardigans, men with unruly facial hair and glasses. I had heard that one of my colleagues was once a homeless man. Now he had a long red beard and no plans to complete his dissertation. He joked about being unmanned by the microwave, offered me herbal teas.

Times were tough and the administration had shunted together the philosophy adjuncts with the English lecturers and comp instructors, and there was a subtle war on among the posters: Virginia Woolf facing off against Nietzsche, Joyce against Adorno. We held in common only our disdain for our subjugated status and student papers: "Marijuana should be legalized," one comp instructor said, "so that I won't have to read another paper about it."

Kate jokingly referred to this state of affairs as the Pedagogy of the Depressed. It's the reason she left academia. Maybe it's the reason I've stayed. Despair can arrest action: I didn't act; I only thought about it. That is, until I met Kate's new friend, Jake.

KATE INTRODUCED US about a week after I returned from the APA conference. We were leaving her office when he came over to say goodnight. He was wearing a peach-colored sweater, something suggested—Kate would later tell me—by a men's magazine to which he subscribed; his hair was blond, cut in a sloppy shag that seemed meant to say, *I am handsome without trying, I am a free spirit trapped in a day job.* He was taller than me—six foot, I'd guess—with a lanky cowboy's build. He had, of all things, a goatee.

It was dislike at first sight.

He told me his name and offered me his hand. "Kate has told me a lot about you," he said.

"She speaks well of you," I said, taking my hand back.

He smiled with only half his mouth, as if he were too hip to bother with symmetry. While they talked, I observed his languorous slouch, his half-closed eyes, lids drooping as if he were hypnotized by Kate's presence. I wondered if this routine often worked on women. I wondered what Kate saw in him.

"We should have dinner sometime," he said, his voice mellifluous as a late-night jazz announcer's. "The three of us."

I was relieved when Kate said we had to get going, she was starved, relieved to follow her after a brief flurry of goodbyes out the door.

On the drive home, Kate fumed about her day. When we'd first gotten involved five years before, sex had sustained us—we had more sex then than any three couples we knew combined—but over time our bond had become one of mutual indulgence. Sounding board more than sex partner. To be fair, she had a lot to complain about. The new features editor at the paper disliked "girl reporters," so Kate's beat had changed after his arrival. She used to cover environmental stories (illegal sewage dumping, unlawful development, Environmental Impact Statements); lately he'd assigned her coverage of stolen fava beans and cockfights. That week it was the national gay rodeo that was coming to town. For background, Kate wanted to check out a gay country-and-western bar in St. Paul.

"I've invited Jake to come along," she said. "You don't mind, do you?"

"Why should I mind?" I said, knowing that a question is not an answer.

THE TOWNHOUSE COUNTRY BAR was packed when we arrived a little past nine. At first glance it was hard to tell it from any other country-and-western joint, with rough-hewn beams and cross rails enclosing the dance floor, a wooden bar and gambling in back. Men and women in cowboy boots, bolos, chaps, and spurs. But look closer and you noticed the rainbow flag beside the dance floor and that the predictable paintings of cowboys and Indians were actually beefcake pics of shirtless braves and cattlemen with well-oiled pecs beside a poster of k.d.lang, and those meaty cowboys gracefully two-stepping across the dance floor held other meaty cowboys in their arms.

As we leaned on the bar, waiting to order, a spark plug of a man with a handlebar mustache and ten-gallon hat approached and asked Jake to dance.

"I'm afraid I don't know that step," Jake said with an easy smile.

"He's *straight*," Kate shouted over the music.

"Can't blame a boy for trying," the cowboy winked, tipped his hat, disappeared in the crowd.

Around us a few people laughed in a nice way. And I began to like Jake just a little. His ease in what some might find an uneasy circumstance.

We found a table near the dance floor, a high, small, round table, the sort of impractical table dance bars favor in order to discourage patrons from staying seated too long. We commandeered three stools and leaned our heads together to be heard over the music.

Jake told us ranching jokes and rodeo tales from the West. He told us that in Salt Lake City they serve a beer called Polygamy Porter, whose label features a naked man embracing seven naked women and the slogan *Why Have Just One?*

"The thing is," he said, smiling, "They'll only serve you one beer at a time. It's illegal to have more than one drink per customer on a table."

"Oh, it has a moral," Kate said. "I love an anecdote with a moral."

We laughed and, despite myself, I warmed to him. He had the appeal of the American West, a boastful self-contentment, an optimism and physical vigor that seemed at once decadent and innocent. It seemed to me that he had something like the delight that animals must take in themselves, a simple pleasure in the body, in life, which I had once taken in life too.

It turned out that Jake, like Kate, had been getting a PhD when he gave it up for journalism. "I don't believe in knowledge for knowledge's sake," he said. "It has to be applied."

"That's what I tell my students," I said.

"A man after your own heart," Kate said.

"So Kate tells me you're a philosopher," he shouted, when Kate went to get some more drinks.

"I teach philosophy. Just the basics: Platonic Forms, the Poetics, Ethics 101."

"So tell me," he leaned close enough that I could smell his faint cologne. "What exactly was the Greeks' position on sex?" He smiled his half smile.

I felt a charge pass between us, a thrill of desire.

"They had a lot of positions," I said, dismissing the question.

He laughed. "Is that a pun?"

"Not at all."

I looked away, watching the dancers on the floor, men in one another's arms.

When Kate returned, we drank another round, shouting over the music, but all I would remember later of that conversation was the heat between me and him, the pressure like a hand on my chest, real as the railroad ties that enclosed the dance floor.

If Kate noticed, she gave no sign.

"I'm going to go snoop around," she said. "You two okay here?"

"We're fine," he said.

"Hurry back," I said. But she was gone already into the crowd and we were left alone together, with the shock of desire arcing between us like a downed live wire and the awareness that whatever we said, we were saying something else.

THE SEMESTER THAT Jake came into our lives, I was teaching two extension classes at the local branch of the state university: Introduction to Platonic Thought, from 3:30 to 4:45 Mondays and Wednesdays, and Ethics 101 on Thursday nights. I had eight students in each, which was just enough to ensure that the administration could not cancel. Enrollment is often spotty and sometimes my classes do not make and I have to pick up a class in composition or the dreaded Study Skills, in which underprepared students work through a softback manual comprising drills on procrastination and time management. I try to be philosophical about it. I take what I can get.

The extension classes with catchy titles do best: Love Among the Runes—which purports to teach students "to divine one's destiny by casting ancient runes" (which are, in fact, brand-new, American-made, plastic bits with faux Norse symbols pressed into their surface)—always has a waiting list. So does Introduction to Astrology. There is a brisk trade in divination these days—astrological columns, palm readings—people seem less interested in preparatory contemplation than in foreknowledge, which seems to me to have it backward.

After all, what good is knowing what's to come if you're ill prepared to cope with it?

WE BEGAN TO SEE a lot of Jake. We became a threesome. He dragged us out to obscure Mexican joints in what passes for a barrio in the Midwest, insisted we canoe from Minneapolis to St. Paul by way of a chain of city lakes. We went to foreign movies: Ken Loach films that required subtitles; a film by Von Trier that required Dramamine; Almodóvar. And each time we met, I felt more acutely the tension between us, like a private joke we were keeping from Kate. I noticed that he took care not to brush my hand when handling the canoe in a portage; he no longer shook my hand in greeting as he had done before. I began to think about him more and more, to find myself distracted by thoughts of him. Things he'd said. To feel an embarrassingly adolescent thrill whenever Kate came home with stories about Jake from work, whenever he called.

I had thought he was gay when we first met, but the thought had passed. Now I asked Kate as we sat reading on the couch one night; she seemed not to have considered it.

"I don't think so," she said, continuing to flip pages in the *Nation*, "but I can see what you mean, I guess. The peach sweater."

"And the goatee," I said.

"Goatees are gay?" she asked.

"They're defensive," I said. "All beards are an assertion of masculinity. Goatees are lowercase masculinity. Ambivalent."

"Where do you get this stuff?" she asked.

"I make it up," I said. "To amuse you."

I considered, abstractly, the possibility of having an affair with Jake—but I dismissed it. I didn't reject the idea on moral grounds. Morality, in my opinion, is overrated, especially in the American empire. "Morality," as Adorno says, "may well appear self-evident to those who feel themselves to be exponents of a class in the ascendent," but for those of us who see little correlation between being powerful and being good, the issue was not so simple.

I didn't believe in monogamy. I remembered a drive that Kate and I had taken once along the shore of Lake Superior; we had driven past pine forests and root beer–colored waterfalls, waves breaking on the rocky shoreline, the sky overhead huge and swirled with cirrus clouds, and I had felt an almost painful joy. I'd reached out and pressed her hand with mine and said "I love you," and in that moment knew for the first time that what I meant when I said that was "I love *all* of this." And that to try to compress that joy and that desire into a single love is a kind of mutilation of spirit.

Honesty restrained me instead: Kate and I were scrupulously frank with one another. I wanted to discuss my crush with her, but something prevented me. Maybe it was a recognition that Jake was her friend, or that he was a man, or that mine was more than the usual attraction. In any case, I didn't mention it.

WE'D BEEN SEEING Jake regularly for several months when we went to the U film society to see *Vanya on Forty-second Street*, a film about a cast of actors rehearsing a Chekhov play and the sexual intrigues among them. I was trying to keep my mind on the movie, off of him, when I put my arm around Kate and my hand landed on his shoulder by mistake, and we both started.

"Shhh," Kate said, setting her hand high on my thigh, nuzzling her head against me.

I looked over at him, his profile flashing in the light from the screen, his eyes forward, refusing to meet mine.

At home that night, I told Kate that it would be better if they went out without me from now on. I told her that I had too much work these days to join them, that I found him a little tiresome.

"You never like my friends," she said.

"Don't be ridiculous," I said. "You don't have any friends." I regretted it as soon as I'd said it, but it was too late to take it back.

To my surprise, Kate laughed.

"You're right," she said. "I don't like many people. That's why I wish you liked Jake."

I told her that I did, that I was just preoccupied.

She leaned up and kissed me. "A misanthrope and a hermit, we make a great pair."

When he came by after that, I contrived to go out. When they went out, I stayed in. I heard through Kate that he often asked after me; he asked her if I played racquetball, said he'd like to play a game with me sometime, if she didn't mind. She said she'd pass on the message; I told her I'd rather not. I avoided her office, picked her up at the curb.

I still thought about him, but I thought about him less.

IN CLASS, I often tell my students stories. Stories, I'm convinced, are what we remember, how we learn. Stories, like education, are a species of seduction: seducing students to care about something other than themselves. Drawing them out of their assumptions into a world of surprise.

That term, I began the class with the story of Zeno of Elea and his famous paradoxes. The fifth-century philosopher is not properly a subject for a course in ethics, but his paradox of the arrow is a favorite story of mine so I told it anyway (such are the prerogatives of the pedant). Zeno pointed out that, if one reasons it through, one will see that an arrow shot at a target will never arrive: it will always be half the remaining distance to its goal (given that an object moving from one place to another must first move half the distance toward its goal, then half that distance, et cetera, he demonstrated that an arrow can never reach its mark). If you think about it, you can't get there from here. And yet we do. The arrow pierces the target, defying logic.

Zeno told the story to demonstrate the illusory nature of change by demonstrating the contradiction inherent in any description of motion. I told it to get my students to test philosophical assertions against the world in which they live.

The whole point of an education, as I see it, is to help you take the world personally, to put you on a first-name basis with the culture. But most of my students seem to think that a college education is an extension of adolescence, the intellectual equivalent of training wheels; they live in a state of semiadulthood, while parents foot the bill. When I asked one young woman recently what she was majoring in, she looked at me with frank disdain, as if choices were for losers, and said, with a shrug, "Y'know, pre-life." Life in the academy, my students seem to think, is not the real thing. This is practice. This is only life in theory.

IN EARLY MARCH, Jake heard from his landlord that his building had been sold and that he had thirty days to move, so Kate and I agreed to help him. The morning was wet and soggy with melting. As we walked up the steps to his building, I smelled the heavy scent of wild mushrooms. We were making good time, shuttling boxes down stairs, until Jake and I found ourselves alone in his apartment. The pale March light poured through the French doors from the balcony and the room was very still.

"You've been avoiding me," he said.

I picked up a box. "I'm not avoiding you."

"What have I done?"

"Nothing," I laughed and pushed past him.

He caught my arm. "I must have done something."

"No," I said. "You haven't done anything. It's what I don't want to do."

He didn't ask me to explain. He raised his hand as if he meant to touch my face, when Kate walked in and we both stepped back. I joked that we were the prime movers unmoving. Kate said she didn't know how prime we were but we'd better move, because she wasn't doing this by herself. Afterwards, we went to Jake's new place for pizza and beer. The two of them talked and joked, while I maintained an uncompanionable silence.

On our way home, Kate was cross. She asked why I couldn't be nice to Jake, why I had to be so difficult. I watched the sparkling of the streetlights, like orange emergency flares going up one after another. I felt the terrible weight of regret that sometimes heralds a loss. I told her, as gently as I could, that I was attracted to him, that I loved her but was attracted to Jake. She must have sensed that this was not our usual talk about infatuation. My mouth felt dry.

"Have you fucked him?" her voice was steady, emotionless, the tone she used to use in a heated seminar debate.

I shook my head. "Don't be ridiculous."

"But you want to?"

"Look," I said. "I don't understand it myself. I love you. This has nothing to do with us."

I wanted her to understand that it was like a philosophy problem. A question I needed answered: I wanted to understand what was between me and him. Early on, Kate and I had agreed that we didn't want ours to become a small love, the sort of love we saw all around us, resentful, limiting, couples whose lives were less for all the sacrifices they'd made for the other. Guys who'd given up mountain climbing, women who'd given up jobs or ambitions. We promised each other we'd never be like that. But lately I'd had my doubts about us, and my attraction to him worked on those.

She asked if he felt the same way.

I told her that I thought he did.

We were quiet for a while.

"The heart has its reasons," I said, quoting Pascal, "which reason knows nothing of."

"You're so full of shit," Kate said.

When I woke in the night I heard her crying beside me. In the morning I told her that I wouldn't see him again. And for a while, that seemed to be enough.

THE PHILOSOPHER Iris Murdoch once called marriage a "long conversation," but before I met Kate I treated my love affairs more like a drawn-out argument in which my task was to disprove the premise that ours was a viable relationship. I treated love like a suspect premise to be tested. My concept of courtship (a lawyer lover once told me) bore a strong resemblance to moot court.

With Kate, though, I was trying. I had my doubts, of course. But ours were not big problems, though we often fought about small things. Kate wanted us to go on drives in October to watch the leaves turn, to play miniature golf, buy a barbecue, get cable; and while there was nothing inherently sinister about any of these, I was thirty-three at the time and the thought of these diversions made me feel old.

For a while, though, things were better between us than they had been in a long while. We began going to concerts, to plays, and between us there was a new tenderness; we were both making an effort, even if the effort weighed on us a little. Kate suggested we meet in the afternoons for drinks; we made love on the couch, the sunlight pouring in.

When Kate told me that Jake was seeing the "Sex Goddess," a lonely hearts columnist from a local alternative paper who emphasized toys and leather, I was happy for him and happy to find I didn't care.

WHEN I RAN into Jake a month or two later at Kate's office, we were polite.

"You're looking well," he said.

"Actually," I said, smiling, "I look like you."

He laughed.

It was true. We both wore jeans and men's V-neck undershirts and suit coats. He mentioned that his birthday was that weekend, that he'd be spending it alone (things having gone awry with the Goddess). It seemed only reasonable to invite him out for a drink.

"You should never age alone," I said.

I'd forgotten that Kate was going out of town to cover the Polar Plunge in Ely, a fact I recalled only later that night at home. I considered canceling but decided it was better just not to tell her. I didn't want to upset her, and it hardly seemed worth mentioning. It was just a drink, after all. So we met at the Lexington, a bar in St. Paul the three of us had liked, at the irreproachable hour of 7 pm.

We ordered martinis and sat at the bar. We discussed gin preferences. The virtues of a twist versus an olive. Slowly we relaxed. He told me about the Sex Goddess, who turned out to be a former gymnast from Cloquet, a Norwegian Lutheran with blue eyes and an uncannily flexible body. I told him about my latest idea for a *New Yorker* cartoon: "If Philosophers Had Majored in Business," featuring Cartesian Waters: I Drink Therefore I Am; Platonic Girdles: For That Ideal Form; and Ecce Home Furnishings. He laughed, raised his glass: "I drink, therefore I am." I had forgotten how much I liked his company. I forgot the time. By 1 am, it seemed wise to accept his offer of a ride home. It seemed only polite to invite him in.

I made us coffee while he looked at the bookshelves, the volumes of Adorno, Nietzsche, Wittgenstein, Kant, German idealists, English empiricists. When I returned with the coffee, he took the cup then set it aside and asked if I would kiss him. It was a curious locution. He did not ask if he might kiss me, but whether I would kiss him— my volition the issue at hand. And I liked him for this, even though the kiss was bland. Even though I was aware of the hard length of his tongue, the musty gin taste in my mouth, and then I was aware of none of these things, only of the sickening lurch of desire in my stomach, his mouth, his smooth chest.

D ESIRE CONFOUNDS CATEGORIES.

Systems fail us when it comes to matters of the heart. They leave out too much, lead us to false conclusions. We assume instead of knowing. Our only hope is to learn through experience. Kate was the one who reminded me that the phrase "the exception proves the rule," means not *validates* but *tests*. Desire proves love. Tests it. At least exceptional desire does, but isn't desire always exceptional to those engaged in it?

Lesbians are often accused of narcissism—our love of women blamed on a hatred of men or a hatred of our mothers or a thwarted maturation that has locked one in pursuit of an adolescent mirror image of oneself—as if a woman simply loving another woman were inexplicable without reference to aversion or impediment. But this, in my experience, could not be more wrong. I have loved women because they are beautiful, because they are tender or brilliant, because I am moved by them.

When I fall for a man, as I fell for Jake, it is because he reminds me of myself.

T HE NEXT MORNING, while Jake was in the bathroom, I called Kate on her cell phone, just to hear her voice. I told her that I missed her. She told me that I sounded funny. *Was I okay?* "I'm fine," I said. I remembered how she used to say, whenever I was away at a conference, "You can come home now, all is forgiven." I said it to her now. She laughed. "I didn't know there was anything to forgive." I wanted to tell her everything, but I couldn't. And the thought of that made me terribly lonely. I told her that I had to go, that I had a lot of papers to grade. But I didn't work that day. After Jake left, I sat at my desk watching the wind push the leaves around outside.

W HEN KATE RETURNED, I didn't tell her about the drink. But she must have sensed something. She seemed sad, and I felt a great desire to reassure her, because despite what I had done and was about to do, I loved her. My feelings for him, I wanted to tell her, had nothing at all to do with her. I was trying to find out about love, about what it is to be human, I was after evidence, the facts of the heart. Desiring him did not detract from my love for her, any more than reading one book detracts from enjoying another. But I could tell her none of this.

She said she was having trouble at work. Her assignments were less and less relevant. In the last year she had covered a vampire convention of Anne Rice fans at the Hyatt, the theft of the butter bust of the Dairy Queen from the State Fairgrounds, the House Rabbit Society's Easter pageant. What she called "the cultural trivia of a trivial culture."

"We are the Romans," I said.

"Yeah," she said. "Look what happened to them."

Perhaps I only imagined it, with a lover's narcissism, but it seemed to me that the culture egged me on toward an affair with Jake. Everywhere I turned were exhortations to excess, refutations of restraint. Adultery began to seem like the social equivalent of secondhand smoke, a by-product of a culture loath to accept limits. Ford Motors, that quintessentially American company, whose slogan had once been "We're Number One," now boasted "No Boundaries." Bus billboards pledged NO LIMIT credit cards. Hewlett-Packard insisted "Everything Is Possible." As if we needn't choose. As if choices had no consequences.

FOR A FEW WEEKS Jake and I met at his apartment in the afternoon and made love. I told Kate that I had student conferences, classes to prepare. Our meetings were largely wordless, a matter of gestures—mouths and hands, taste and touch. For hours after leaving him, I was conscious of my skin, dazed with arousal. Familiar streets took on a new brilliancy, the sky a new radiance; as I walked home along Garfield, each house, each sign seemed to possess a new significance.

But the more I desired Jake, the less we had to say to each other. Grasping at desire, it seemed to disappear. After sex, I dressed quickly, eager to get home to Kate. I began to feel closer to her, more tender, protective. I began to notice little things she'd like—a Freud action figure, a biscotti recipe, books on Irish history. I recalled how Kate's stories had amazed me when we first met—stories of her work with the antiapartheid group the Black Sash, of her visits to remote villages and appearances before pink-faced judges to protest pass laws, of her uncle's strangulation by wire, of the taste of blood oranges and olives eaten on a mountain hike. How she had wanted to be an Anglican priest because she liked the phrase "Peace be with you," passed around like a collection plate at the end of every service. I admired how she'd taken part in what Adorno termed "resistance," a refusal "to be part of the prevailing evil, a refusal that always implies resisting something stronger and hence always contains an element of despair." She seemed to carry in her the parched landscape of southern Africa, its desolation and its harsh beauty. I realized that the passion I felt for Jake was passing: our sex was a little like getting drunk, liberating at first but tedious if done too often. I was embarrassed by the boredom I felt.

A month passed and another, before I admitted to Jake that I didn't know if I could do this anymore; he appeared neither disappointed nor surprised. He simply asked if I wanted him to change my mind. I said it would be easy, but that I'd rather he didn't.

And sitting there beside him, I missed him. More than missing him, I missed desiring him.

Kierkegaard—the failed lover—spoke of "the enthusiasm of a love that ever seeks solitude," and I wonder now if this wasn't the source of my disappointment in that affair. What I was seeking with Jake, I suspect, wasn't him—lovely as he was—but a more perfect solitude, a more complete sense of the world. I wanted the feeling that comes when you release yourself toward things—reading can do this, and looking at a painting, and listening to music, or walking through half-empty streets almost anywhere alone at night will do this. I wanted to stand in the radiant presence of desire, when all things, the black branches of trees, light falling on brick, the strains of a violin concerto, one's own hand, seem illuminated by a loveliness musical in its intensity.

WHEN JAKE CALLED my office a few days after we ended our affair, I was surprised. He asked to meet at a pub in St. Paul. He sounded nervous; I noted that he didn't suggest we meet at his apartment.

When I arrived he was waiting in a booth. We ordered beers, chatted awkwardly.

"Have you run across my sweater," he asked. "The peach one?"

"I thought you'd thrown it over for a tweed," I said. I had not seen the sweater in weeks.

He didn't laugh.

"I've checked my car," he said. "I can't find it. I thought maybe."

"I'll check."

We drank pints of ale, and he flirted with the waitress, and it was clear that whatever had been between us was over now.

KATE WAS THE ONE who found the coral sweater. The hideous thing had fallen behind the radiator in our bedroom, cast off, evidently, without attention. When she told me, I blushed, stammered. Confused by the implication, which—until she saw my reaction—she had not seen. When she asked me directly what was going on, if I'd slept with him, I couldn't bring myself to lie.

Kate sat on the couch and covered her face and cried as if someone she'd loved had died. And I started to cry, too. And it occurred to me that in all my careful reasoning I had left out one key thing: empathy. My formulation of the problem had been wrong, the premise flawed. I had been so concerned with the true and the untrue, the ethical versus the moral, action and inaction, that I had failed to consider the obvious, the simple fact that I might hurt the woman I loved.

I told her that it had nothing to do with us. That it was over.

"You're right," she said, standing. "It is." And she walked out.

FOR A WHILE Kate and I tried to patch things up. We got back together. Made love. Fought. Cried. Called it off and on again for a couple of months. Until finally we no longer remembered what it was we were trying to save, a time before things were over. I heard that Jake left the paper a few months later to return to school. I did not see him again.

Even now I prefer to think of ours as a temporary separation, not an ending. I take comfort in the thought that things haven't really changed, that Kate's absence is a momentary break, which time will heal—that change, as Zeno would have it, is illusory.

But every so often I remember the story in PMS of the follower of Zeno who was lecturing before a crowd in Athens, gesticulating wildly as he made his points. The Zenoist was arguing that an object cannot move, because it cannot be in more than one place at a time. "If it moves where it is, it is standing still. If it is where it is not, it cannot be there," he said, when suddenly he dislocated his shoulder. A doctor was called from the crowd. Asked to fix the shoulder, the physician explained that it could not be dislocated: either the shoulder was where it had been and was not dislocated, or it had moved to where it was not, which was impossible. At which point the patient saw what should have been obvious all along: Logic can mislead us. If we rely on reason alone, the answers we seek may elude us.

I remembered the story this morning as I watched my students write their midterm exams. It is one of those extraordinarily windy days in autumn and all manner of things were blowing past the classroom window, the flotsam of other lives—pages of newsprint, plastic bags like round white kites, twigs and cups and colored flyers—and in the midst of the maelstrom, I saw something go by, out of the corner of my eye, which must have been a twig, but which looked like a child's arrow, and I thought briefly that it could be one of Cupid's, or Zeno's—aiming for something it will never, ever, reach.

To Summer

I'll admit I looked forward to your departure,
the end of the heat wave, the black spit
of Mulberry, the last of our best goblets
dashed. Right now you are speeding, leaving
the north road, shedding the threaded vineyards,
the herb and goat farms, each numbered exit
closing the gap between you and your syllabus,
our school year apart. Mack trucks race, freighted
like you, with obligations. Already, I wish
it were May and you, with your good reasons
for quitting the job, stood in the yard, your bike
still bolted to its rack. I wish we were now
pulling on our suits. You, with your long legs,
your never veering attention to my faults.
Maybe my virtues will swim to the surface when you,
with your open-to-be-thwarted heart, come back.

DANIEL HALL

At the Nursery

for my mother

The end of May's already hot as Hades.
Ranks of saplings, pine and maple,
up on tiptoe, gawky and hopeful,
spatter the gravel with watery shade.
Beyond the chainlink, life goes on
for free, too far or too familiar
even to notice: the run-of-the-mill
varieties, wind-lashed, whisper and moan
as they have done, as they will always do.
I think of
            —then can't think of you,
can't think at all, fixed by the stare
of a warbler perched six feet away from me,
a thousand miles from its native tree,
late, weeks late, and desperate to be there.

Roosters

One sounds like he's just beginning to crow after an adolescence
dancing or harrying the hens or thinking perhaps he was a hen.
What was the difference between them, really? Just a hairsbreadth comb
placed fleshily on the crack of his cranium, odd as a single labium, alert,
sunburned, now unaccountably growing. Is this the flag of roosterhood,
or is it these tailfeathers black and green as certain inks?

In these past two days, he feels the need for voice, for practice
though he has nothing important to announce. Oh, the sunrise, yes,
but also the damp place in the dirt asquirm with insect life, the hose left
snaking out uncoiled all night. He heralds twilight. He sounds mammalian,
not quite car-hit dog, not child being maimed, not cat rent by feline
passion, but some new sound breaking out of its membrane.

Carmen and her cousin have not spoken for three years over a trivial
misunderstanding that might have been avoided had either been willing
to change her position. Then Carmen broke up with her girlfriend.
Then her mother's leg was cut off due to diabetes, infection, and gangrene.
They, too, had been estranged, but Carmen rushed to her mother's bed.
Her mother said she'd have given both legs to have Carmen back again.

The photos of myself taken just a day ago for the immigration forms
already seem alien, as blood seems once it is drawn from the vein
and bagged in plastic and labeled with black pen. Though it is still warm
from my body, it soon chills, mixed with a salt, and laid unceremoniously
on a shelf. I'm lonely for that self, hours old, stilled and fraught with
secret meanings, where I sat on a stool exposed and faintly ridiculous.

Yet the woman didn't care who I was as she slapped the cold roll of film
into her camera. She just wanted my shoulders straight, my chin up,
my eyes not to close. But when I look at the blotchy skin of my cheeks,
my sunburned nose, I see my whole family, a grandmother I didn't know,

her profile like my profile, the small chin with its wattle of skin below,
the slumped shoulders and neck thrust unagressively forward.

I want to be loved in that posture, to be found handsome even though
my heavy breasts pull me down and the hours I spend at my desk
make my shoulders slope. Like everyone else, I want to be adored.
I still carry such foolish, unquenchable hope. That tousled haircut
and green cotton shirt are not me though I did sit there for a moment.
She is contained, that woman with the lined neck, but I have flown out.

MARY ANN McFADDEN

San Ignacio Lagoon, Clear Water

After a while we could recognize a whale under the boat, or in the near
distance by the pale mass, sometimes moving, sometimes still,

but we couldn't tell how deep it was or what it might do next.

There was an immanence, a barely perceptible bulge or heave
in the imagination or in the sea, it was hard to tell which was which
from our small craft, and after a while our longing was such
that it didn't matter anyway.

With us were two young people, a couple more fixed
on each other than on anything else. They had discovered sex,

invented it actually, and were so caught in their mutual
fascination that the rest of the world was dull,

even this most remarkable hour they might ever pass.

You and I have lived long enough to know that the erotic
has a life apart from its participants, that it can move away from us

and return just as surprisingly, and that we are no more in control
of its comings and goings than we are of the weather. We know,

or think we know what to do, the way a nun lights candles,
dresses ritually in the cold and makes her way to the sanctuary.

She falls on her knees and begins the loved movements of mind, tongue, throat, hands. Yet grace, when it comes, is still a mystery.

We can seek, but we cannot find.

The Crisis

Unwilling to be dragged through a marriage any longer.

Was equilibrium what we were ever after?

A stasis bridging the dual abyss?

Never mind that carousel on which we endlessly ride.

Hip flab hanging off forty-something hags.

Nothing sadder than a clown fingering dirty bills.

Our toddlers in line ripped off

Rolling blackouts said to be expected all summer long.

The Marriage

Spent more time at the opera than on those he loved.

Affliction gawking at paid admission.

As ever he'd been looking for someone to blame.

Ill effects of hurry on the tissues.

Tiles made out of fossilized ferns installed in the vestibule.

Love duplicating the key's toothed steel.

Whispered back and forth without forgiveness.

Hence the steady decline.

Sordid ghosts caught inside the door-dwell of an Otis.

Shadow-Land

To pass
steadily, patient, ever-wanting out of
one darkness, and into a next one, and again
out: so a life is made—not the worst one;
perhaps the only one, around which
what had looked original or like some
chance-of-escape
exception has been so much ringing
of changes on a theme
we've heard. Who can say? But this time the dark
is more dark than any I've known
before, and I've know many. At each, I've taken
leave as if leave-taking were itself
souvenir—as, in the end, it seems, it
will have had to be. The rest may as well

be writ on a memory even I wouldn't trust
too far, not as
unwaveringly, at least, as I trust
my ability to make distinctions that
still matter, here, if only to me: the openness
I call the sea is not that openness that I once called
ocean, for example; or
there's a distance, a very real one, between
granting to no one especially and
withholding from all concerned parties equally
one's body first, then something less
tangible, not tangible at all, that
somehow counts more. One saw that, one
eventually came to . . . There's a cover-of-night
part of me,

inside me, that remembers exactly how I became
—what I've become. A silence falls there,
in that darkness, sometimes like a first falling
crop of snow, sometimes like the reverse
of when the singer, having found
the one note at last worth holding onto, begins
lifting it; and the crowd, whose gift it is—no, whose
best instinct is
to know a gift when it hears one—follows,
as a crowd is meant to. There are rules. They were
there from the start. There are those who,
when they love a thing, must break it first, in order that
the beloved require them
more absolutely, don't you know me
by now?

RENAISSANCE MINDSCAPE

I HAVE ALWAYS been drawn to Renaissance art, particularly to Renaissance portraits. These paintings are a result of my exploration with portraiture and self-portraiture coupled with my love for Renaissance imagery. Throughout my painting career I have explored portraiture and self-portraiture working with costume and face painting. When I first began, I developed a series of head self-portraits in which my face was completely painted into patterns. As I worked, I became increasingly interested in the patterns and what they evoked as opposed to the conventional rendition of facial features. Eventually, I eliminated the facial features and expressions and used only the outline of the face to represent a thought or feeling. This stimulated my exploration further, which in turn led me to develop this "Renaissance Mindscape" series.

In this group of paintings, I reinterpret 16th and 17th century Renaissance portraits by omitting the subject's facial features while working within the outline of the face itself. Instead of facial features I paint an image symbolizing a momentary "mindscape." This "mindscape" is my interpretation of a moment in the sitter's emotional state. These "mindscapes" are not meant to lock the sitter into a particular mood or setting. Instead, they are meant to represent a thought, a state of mind or a feeling much like the ones we all experience consciously and subconsciously.

ROXA SMITH

NEW WORLD, 2002

ESCAPE, 2001

LABOR, 2002

EXPLORER, 2004

ISOLATION, 2004

ANGUISH, 2003

SANCTUARY, 2004

PORTRAITS

R EPRESENTATIONAL PAINTING often carries the burden of realism. Realism, as a formal principle, can be misunderstood as a technique that "uncovers truth" through observation. My interest in realism is to demonstrate the contrary. I emphasize the fabricated or superficial/artificial components of my subjects. Fantasy determines the clothes/props we wear, as we sort out the person we are, and want to be. Often, identities are multiple, and sometimes even in conflict. Clothing, and the ability to change it, permits a form of "serial identity." The "Angie" paintings, for example, are named after her lipstick choices. In my work, covering is revealing—there is no naked truth. I work with models in my studio, and I involve my models in my process. Because each model is different each series of work demands a different strategy.

I employ a fairly conventional form of art—observational figure painting, and do so to position the work within a tradition of painterly dicta and conventions. I think of myself as a formalist who calls attention to the "made-upness" of form. I manipulate both the formal and conceptual elements in my work. One convention of portrait painting is the manipulation or construction of the psychology of the sitter. The psychology of these paintings is not fixed; it develops out of my relationship with the sitters and then is elaborated or transformed by the viewer. There is no naked truth.

TIM DOUD

KAREN (FUR COAT), 2002

ANGIE (WANDERLUST), 2001

ANGIE (RUBY WOO), 2002

ANGIE (CHICKORY), 2003

Private collection, Den Haag, The Netherlands. Courtesy Galerie Brusberg Berlin.

ANGIE (POLLY VINYL), 2002

ANGIE (PINK POODLE), 2001

STUD DRESS, 2002

CLIFFORD CHASE

The Tooth Fairy

NEW YORK

Fat little dog trotting contentedly along the sidewalk, right at his master's side, with a plastic steak in his mouth.

Neil Young sounds like a lonely alley cat, most poignant when slightly out of tune.

Whenever I get on the subway, I look around for someone cute to glance at, and if there isn't anyone I resign myself to boredom.

Old queen in the locker room: "When you're the prettiest one in the steam room, it's time to go home."

Aphorism-like statements, when added one to another, might accrue to make some larger statement that might placate despair.

At forty-three I'm no longer in my heyday.

The name of the medication printed in a half-circle and the "100 mg." make a smiley face on my new, blue pills.

On the L train, a poem called "Hunger" speaks of walking home "through a forest that covers the world."

I've had the same part-time public relations job for nearly sixteen years.

I'm drawn to Neil Young at the moment not by the specific content of the lyrics (too hetero) but by the overall tone of longing, which I define as a kind of sadness that has hope.

On the L platform, a diminutive Chinese man playing "Send in the Clowns" on a harmonica, to flowery recorded accompaniment.

The intensity of certain random experiences is sometimes unaccountable and makes one wish to live more observantly.

I'd hoped to overcome negative thinking through therapy, meditation, prayer, swimming, and yoga, but now it appears I also need a drug.

According to WebMD, Wellbutrin carries a risk of seizure.

The problem with polyester is that it pills, yet sometimes it doesn't, and you can never tell which it will be.

After eight years my boyfriend and I still don't live together, and I wonder if this is a failure.

I thought, "Let the seizure come, and maybe afterwards I'll have some peace."

I support myself mostly with public relations writing rather than journalism because public relations writing is always positive, and I like to be nice.

In his spare time, my ophthalmologist is an amateur magician.

I went to look at the sunset and was given a ticket for trespassing.

My arthritis has been bad this week, but I hope that if I think of myself as a well person rather than a sick one, the pain will bother me less and less and might even go away.

"Colors were brighter," says a woman of her first week on Effexor, which I also tried but didn't like.

My Walkman in my breast pocket, I floated along with the sad tune.

The ronroco, a small Argentine string instrument, sounds like a cross between a ukulele and a mandolin.

In an e-mail regarding the freelance article I was working on, the marketing executive at Jordache tried to flirt with me by offering vintage jeans and asking my waist size.

I like Internet porn too much.

Mae West makes odd, inarticulate, knowing "humph" sounds, sometimes barely audible, and when she "dances," she barely moves.

I wrote that the old 1979 Jordache commercial, which was being shown again on TV, "begins with a downward glissando," a line my editor took out, even though that glissando is my favorite part of the ad.

Joni Mitchell once wisely observed that disco music sounded like typewriters.

My editor also cut: "We only glimpse the blond girl dancing, in a manner not seen since, say, the New York City Gay Pride Parade in 1989, that is, as if her shoulders are attached to one circular track and her hips to another."

I've noticed that whenever I trim my sideburns, I think of a particular editor I barely know, and since I like her I don't mind thinking of her while shaving, but sometimes I would like to know, Why her?

For another article I spent my day off in Staten Island interviewing once again the teenager with HIV I had interviewed two and a half years ago.

My therapist of twelve years almost started crying as she spoke of another patient, a priest, who died of AIDS.

I went in search of a black version of the navy blue cotton-polyester polo shirt I'd seen at Bloomingdale's, and I found it at Saks.

Though my brother died of AIDS and we had discussed this many times, I had never seen my therapist cry before.

As soon as I switched from Effexor to Wellbutrin, my orgasm returned.

The colors of some moments are slightly brighter than others, and some a lot brighter, and at the moment I'm interested in those just slightly brighter.

I love blood oranges.

I went home and tried on all my new clothes.

My boyfriend said I'm like that dog with his plastic steak when I have a new shirt to wear.

Articles I could write for *GQ:* "Searching for the Perfect Black Polo Shirt"; "Shoe Shopping with My Podiatrist"; "How Can You Tell If a Particular Polyester Blend Will Pill?"; "Why Do Certain Flat-Front Pants Wrinkle So Much in the Crotch?"

I was thinking of leaving my therapist and even went to see three new candidates but decided I would only reach the same point with a new one eventually anyway, for reasons that are officially known as "resistance" and "transference" and which, in practical terms, mean I've been afraid to go forward.

My mother and father like to playfully call milk "malk" and cooking "coo-king."

Similarly, my boyfriend and I repeat the same phrases again and again, phrases from movies or life that made us laugh, as when John overheard a fag in a coffee shop say, apparently of his boyfriend, "I don't know *where* she is, I don't know if she's got a *dick* in her mouth . . ."

When you feel a strong connection to your therapist, not only do you mistake her for your mother, but she sort of really *is* your mother, because she has taught you that much.

In an e-mail my friend Cathy, who is legally blind, explained to me for the first time in our twenty-two-year friendship exactly what she sees, that is, a rapid series of blurry snapshots, because her eyes won't hold still.

I begged off having a drink with the boss, saying I had dinner plans, which was true: I had planned to have dinner with myself.

I said I couldn't have lunch with the salespeople tomorrow because there was something I had to do, which was true: I had to be alone.

Things I like to do on Wellbutrin: blow my boyfriend, lie in bed switching channels, write one-sentence paragraphs, not get mad at store clerks, masturbate, read stereo-equipment catalogs, plan to go to Rome.

Soaked through after walking only half a block, I said to myself, "This weather is absurd. Absurd!"

I'm discouraged to discover that certain childhood experiences continue to wreck my life, and so I must look at them one more time.

Subway graffiti: "Admit when your gay and a slacker."

I've been writing a novel about my teddy bear, in part, I suppose, because I'm perpetually in need of comfort.

Driving me back to the ferry, the grandmother of the kid with HIV said wryly, as we passed the hospital, "There it is, our home away from home."

I told my therapist that when she nearly cried, I thought she might be telling me she was too fragile to be my therapist, but she replied that that wasn't the case.

On the telephone John and I try to imitate Mae West's inarticulate humphs, but since they're nearly inaudible, our imitations aren't much of a success.

When I took my trespassing ticket to 346 Broadway, they said I had come on the wrong day.

In Union Square station, a teen to a fellow teen: "You sound like a fucking hibernating bear. Maybe you should sleep six months and shit."

Moments of a certain off flavor add up, and then you perceive you're in a new phase of your life.

If there's a pattern here, I can't see it.

In my teddy bear novel I will have to write about shitting my pants all the time when I was five, and I'm not sure how to go about describing that.

After eight years I relate to John very well within certain parameters, and we're working to expand those parameters, but sometimes I'm afraid I'm not up to the challenge and cannot change.

My dentist pointed to a small dark area on the X-ray.

On the phone John read me a funny article about Kathy Lee Gifford.

There are certain moments and facts the mind returns to, for whatever reason.

I stared out my office window.

There was nothing more to be done for the tooth, so I would have to have it pulled, and it would have to be done now, before I went to Rome.

Young subway cop, tubby and all in blue, standing by the token booth vigorously chewing his nails.

Doesn't Dante refer to middle age as a "forest"?

"You may hear a cracking sound," said the oral surgeon, who is also named Cliff. He was inserting a pair of pliers in my mouth. I heard the cracking. Occasionally life plunges you into an experience which, for its utter intensity and obscure resonance, may as well be a dream. "You doin' OK?" Cliff asked. "Uh-huh," I tried to say, though actually even after the five or six shots of Novocain I still had some sensation in one spot on my gum, but that was too difficult to explain. My mouth was propped open by a black plastic brace, which I bit down on with my left teeth, the side he wasn't working on. Cliff said, "You're going to feel some vibration." I glimpsed the instrument before it went in. I wondered if he wished I'd opted for the Valium and Demerol, so then he wouldn't have to explain everything he was doing. However, he was good at explaining. I felt the high-pitched vibration of the power tool (drill? tiny saw?). Then the tugging of the pliers, as the gray-haired, German-accented assistant gently but firmly—Germanly, I thought—held my chin in place. More tugging. This went on for a while, the power tool, then the pliers, first one root, then the other. I kept my eyes closed and the light on my eyelids was bright as daylight. I tried to imagine I was at the beach. Again and again my shoulders tensed up and I would have to remember to relax them. To describe this ordeal as primal might be misleading, since I was too deep in the woods of it to describe it to myself at all. If I were to interpret, I might say it confirmed a nameless and fundamental conviction that life had stolen something nameless and fundamental from me. This might also be called the human condition, but like the protagonist in a dream I was exempt, for the time being, from drawing any such conclusions. At last there was a final tug which, though I could see nothing, seemed decisive and was. He dropped the pliers in the metal tray with a clang.

Just as I switched the channel to Jenny Jones, she said, "So, you have sex for money. And you work at White Castle?"

Mouth full of gauze, I had to stop by the office because the goddamn FedEx package hadn't arrived the day before.

On the subway stairs: "If I hear any more about your anger management class, I'm going to throw up."

A fever after a tooth extraction is normal.

I began seeing flashing lights on the periphery of my left eye, so I called my magician-ophthalmologist, who told me I have Foster Moore's Lighting Flashes, a harmless condition that can affect near-sighted people in middle age.

Apparently Barbara Stanwyck once said "Fuck you" to Loretta Young.

I tried to participate in my oral surgeon's manful matter-of-factness, but I still mourn the molar, designated Number 30.

I broke down when my therapist said she felt outrage for certain things I had suffered as a child.

Cliff had also been my oral surgeon more than fifteen years earlier, on this very same tooth, which that time was saved, and that time I did do the Valium and Demerol, and I remember Cliff trying to wake me up by calling my name, which of course was also his own name, over and over:

". . . Cliff . . . Cliff . . . Cliff . . . Cliff . . . Cliff . . . ? Howyadoin?"

ROME

Perfectly cooked squid is like an extra-firm mattress for the teeth.

"I didn't realize it would be so tarted up," said John in the ancient church that had been redone in the Baroque style.

I love *La Dolce Vita* because rather than making Marcello reform or find himself, it allows him simply to go further into depravity.

"They're so tall!" I said of the many sycamores, which were just getting their leaves.

After a week my tongue grew accustomed to the gap in my molars and even began to caress the gap's edges lovingly.

"That meal will go down in history," I said, taking one last bite.

In exchange for the tooth, at least I had been granted the vivid experience of losing it.

Coming down through the billowing mosaic-clouds: God's hand.

As we ate our gelato we decided we like Rome better than Paris.

Any single moment could be definitive and final, just as the world might end at any moment.

On our archeological tour beneath St. Peter's, the Vatican guide informed us that the early Christians depicted Jesus as the sun: "They didn't know what he looked like then, because that was, of course, before the Shroud of Turin."

I leaned against the refrigerator and it moved, prompting me to remark that Italian refrigerators are lighter than American ones.

Even on vacation John has moments of panicky sadness that I find at once understandable and terrifying.

At dinner we couldn't remember what calculus was, and I said it had something to do with describing a curve with an infinite number of separate points.

In the Vatican Museums, just after the Sistine Chapel, there's a small wooden box marked "Suggestions."

Pouting near the Coliseum, I was reminded strongly of childhood and thought to myself, "Whatever it is I'm feeling, it's very old, so why don't I just put it aside for now?" and indeed somehow I was able to do so.

"I like that game that Gary and Jean played, 'What City Would You Want to Live in If You Could Live Anywhere?'" I said to John, "though I have a feeling they play that game a lot," and John said, "So do we."

As a child I felt only excruciating embarrassment, rather than mirth, when the Beaver got into various scrapes, such as climbing up into a giant teacup on a billboard.

The stairs to our sleeping loft were metal and not very steep, and they clanged cheerfully as we quickly ascended and descended.

In the Caravaggio that made me understand Caravaggio, Doubting Thomas places his finger in the wound in Christ's side, and that wound is like a tear in the painting itself.

John laughed as I sang for him my favorite Stephin Merritt song:

> Papa was a rodeo
> Mama was a rock 'n' roll band
> I could play guitar and rope a steer
> Before I learned to stand
> Home was anywhere with diesel gas
> Love was a trucker's hand . . .

As it turned out, Michelangelo's famous sculpture of Moses was covered in bubble wrap.

The pervasive, calming, cheerful sun.

We realized the delicious sandwiches we had just bought were only a dollar fifty.

Because a child will try to adjust to anything including and especially parental failings, therefore I did play guitar and rope a steer before I learned to stand.

". . . bla bla bla Catherine Zeta-Jones bla bla bla," said the Italian television announcer.

The oranges we bought each day were large, sweet, and just slightly bloody inside.

Bernini's elephant in sunshine.

At the gay-owned shop, I bought John a cunning little pepper grinder for his birthday.

Our two bunches of ranunculi lasted the whole nine days.

The trees streamed past the train window as if they were being sucked up by a vacuum cleaner.

To sit on the aisle, I accepted a seat way in the back, but then the people next to me kept wanting to get up.

I found the in-flight movie almost unbearable because of the many humiliations suffered by the main character.

The sky really does look different everywhere you go.

NEW YORK

In fifth grade I wrote an essay that concluded, "As Plato said, power corrupts."

"I don't know how much longer I can last in corporate America," I muttered, but then I've been saying that for years.

I read that a '70s pop star killed himself with an overdose of amitriptyline; remembered that's the scientific name for what I've been taking for arthritis pain; realized I have options.

On the record albums of my youth, the various aesthetic choices seem so inevitable that they hardly appear to be choices at all, such as when the applause following "The Needle and the Damage Done" is suddenly cut short.

I was hoping that with the help of my blue pills I would either ccase hating my public relations job or be able to find a new one.

On the weather map the clouds were in a slow spin across the continent.

"The Long and Winding Road" made me cry when I was twelve, and ever since then I've loved sad songs.

Without understanding why, this winter I spiraled down into punishing sadness and terror, which manifested themselves most mercilessly on weekday evenings.

Most jobs are nothing more than service with a smile, and then the day is over.

People often tell me, "You're the only one I'm not mad at."

I can only deal with crying every other therapy session.

As I sunk further, I became overwhelmed by even the smallest thing, a state which reminded me of my mother.

I feel guilty when I'm mean to customer service representatives, but I do it anyway.

I think there should be a magazine called *Naked GQ,* which would be exactly the same as *GQ,* only the models would all be naked.

The only problem with my blue pills, as with vacations, is that the same conundrums, of work and love, remain.

I frequently imagined screaming arguments with my boss and with others in management.

I'm reading a book by a hunchback dwarf who died in 1942.

At the party celebrating his twentieth anniversary with the magazine, the editor in chief said, "I tell my kids that if you can find a line of work that you love, then you're truly blessed," and I wrote it down to put in the company newsletter.

I'm ashamed of my life, including the shame itself.

And yet I see in these day-fragments glimmerings of some sort of perspective.

After I wired John money in Tunisia, because his bank card didn't work, I thought, "This is the kind of crisis I'm good at."

I can see the possible literary merit, if not the actual merit, of my current predicament in life.

I love best works of art that are both absurd and moving.

Once a top executive complained to a coworker of mine that there weren't enough blueberries in his muffin.

Riding the subway home from work, I longed to hear Joni sing of being a poor wayfaring stranger.

At least it's spring now.

The magazine's writers have recently published books on baldness; civil rights; cryptography; early American music; an incident of arson in Vail, Colorado; current social and political issues (from a neocon perspective); and how to live "a happy life."

"Major quitting fantasies," I wrote in my journal.

The pale springlike green of my jacket pleased me and I was happy again.

"Sometimes a worm will sew a stitch in a young leaf, and even though the leaf may partly unfold, and partly grow and live, it will always be a crumpled and imperfect leaf. . . . Because the worm had sewed a stitch in me and made me forever crumpled, I belonged to the fantastic company of the queer, the maimed, the unfit."

I learned on the *Today Show* that Valerie Harper's new book is called *Today I'm a Ma'am*, and it's about growing older.

My feet are OK, but my right knee has been bothering me again, who knows why.

I prefer having an easy job that I can do perfectly, rather than a hard job that I can't, because I hate making mistakes.

I hope my yoga teacher likes me.

The geometric pattern in my tin ceiling suddenly looked like gritted teeth.

It's more suave to have no regrets, but I do have them.

I don't look my age, but I've lost my looks anyway.

More boys should take off their shirts in the park.

I had to squeeze through a crowd to reach Psychology, because Valerie Harper was doing a book signing.

See *The Emotional Brain,* by Joseph LeDoux, page 12.

At the top of the subway steps, the blossoming trees were palest green against a pale, green-gray sky.

"I let my socks not matching go too far," said John as he cleaned his apartment, "and now I can't make heads or tails of them."

Ringing in my ears, probably from the Wellbutrin.

My friend David sent me a linocut he made of the Loch Ness Monster.

I began reading a book on the history of Latin America.

My arthritis doctor said, "If you think rheumatology is hit or miss, psychopharmacology is like when I was a little girl and I'd shut my eyes and point to which stuffed animal I wanted to sleep with that night."

In the dream I was listening to a Fifth Dimension sort of song that went:

> Shagga dagga diddly—
> Shagga dagga diddly—
> Doo!

I dreamed Martha Stewart guest-starred on *Love Boat*.

The plot was simple: Martha turned out not to be so uptight after all.

At the end of the show, Martha jumped in the pool with all her clothes on.

Down my street the horizon was bright yellow and the blanket of clouds was soft, yellow and mauve, like a golden cloth with a purple sheen, and soon the pink part began.

I can only hope that the talking cure isn't pointless.

It took all morning, but I didn't have to pay a fine for trespassing.

On the phone my friend Erin said, "I just got a bill from AT&T for forty-six cents, and they're not even my long distance carrier."

". . . He walks slowly, listening alertly because lost souls weep or sometimes whistle like the breeze.

"When he finds the missing soul, the wizard-priest lifts it with the tip of a feather, wraps it in a tiny ball of cotton, and carries it in a little hollow reed back to its owner, who will not die."

I dreamed I was cutting up the American flag into confetti, and even now I can feel the cool scissors in my hand, the sensation of the thick cloth giving way, and the pleasure of it.

Weird how rough a winter I had.

When I lost a baby tooth, Mom had me drop it into a glass of water. I watched the hard little white thing float down to the bottom, and then we placed the glass on the shelf beside my bed. In the morning my tooth was gone, and a dime was in its place. It wasn't exactly a miracle, but it was straightforward and predictable, and it helped mark my progress forward on the earth. This memory, though brief, gives me a warm, happy feeling.

I dreamed I was eating ferns.

> And Lord knows, I spent a long time writing bad poems. I did it as a practice because I wanted to figure out what made a poem bad. It was hard for me to set out to write a good poem and end up with a good poem, but it was pretty easy to set out to write a bad poem and end up with a bad poem.

CHRISTOPHER HENNESSY

Breaking Past
the Margins

AN INTERVIEW WITH D. A. POWELL

D. A. POWELL'S poetry is visceral, often sexual, sometimes disturbing, completely unacademic and irreverent but formal in its own way—and more human than autobiographical. Over the course of three books—*Tea, Lunch,* and *Cocktails,* a trilogy he calls his own *Divine Comedy*—Powell has developed a voice like few others, at turns brazen and sensitive. And with his signature titles—bracketed first lines—and his long but chopped-up breathy lines, Powell seems to have carved out new poetic territory for himself.

The poems in *Tea* (Wesleyan University Press, 1998), his first book, pulsed past the margins of the normal page. "Because I was unable to contain the first line I wrote, I turned my notebook sideways," he writes in the book's introduction. "These lines, with their peculiar leaps and awkward silences, became the strangely apt vessel into which I could pour my thoughts."

"Life is a poor edit . . . clip cut and paste," writes Powell in *Lunch* (Wesleyan, 2000). With a lexical salad bowl and a constantly shifting tone, *Lunch* mines childhood, romance, nostalgia, pop culture, and myth and contains poems that continue to push the limits: "darling can you kill me: with your mickeymouse pillows," says one poem's speaker, pleading to be euthanized.

With *Cocktails* (Graywolf Press, 2004), Powell offers longer, denser, more linguistically exploded poems. His language is witty and full of puns, and moments later cutting and rife with brutal truths— seen, for example, in the dark but beautiful prick (and prick) of his poem "[my lover my phlebotomist . . .] "from the book's first section, entitled "Mixology." Though he continues to work in autobiographical terms, many of these poems are steeped in allegory and allusion. The second section, "Filmography," takes its inspirations from films as various as *The Poseidon Adventure* and *My Beautiful Launderette.* "Bibliography," the final section, contains challenging poems that eerily circle the Gospels while probing our wounds, faith, and ability to love, and how we face mortality.

Powell's awards include the Lyric Poetry Award from the Poetry Society of America, the Larry Levis Award from *Prairie Schooner,* *Boston Review*'s Annual Poetry Award in 2001, and a grant from the National Endowment for the Arts, among others. He's taught at the University of San Francisco, San Francisco State University, Sonoma State University, the University of Iowa, and Columbia University. He is a founding editor of the online journal *Electronic Poetry Review.*

We conducted the interview in his office at Harvard, where he was serving as the Briggs-Copeland Lecturer, in the fall of 2003, a few months before the publication of *Cocktails.*

CH: Many of the poems in your latest book, *Cocktails,* are longer, more complex, and certainly risking more than your previous work. Do the new subjects and themes you're exploring—the poems with religion as theme and image especially seem to risk more—demand that you're structurally and imaginatively extending, pushing the poems?

DAP: I did want to push beyond what I would normally consider the boundary of a poem. What happens when you feel like you've reached an end but have to continue? It's what I do with periods. I use periods as full stops, but then I push past them to say that this is not just an ending, it's a connective—to frustrate the normal sense of what constitutes closure. By pushing beyond what would feel like the end of the poem, I wanted to open up the subject more; I felt that there might be an opportunity for more discovery. Also, there are moments in these poems where syntax goes completely out the window, where there really are just words bursting in these self-contained little bubbles. In some cases, meaning is carried by the sound, and in some cases, by the referents of the work, but I like the fact that the sentence gets abandoned completely. I'm not much interested in sentences as a poet to begin with, and it's wonderful when you can just have words be words, in and of themselves. I like [Gertrude] Stein because she takes words completely out of context and listens to their music and the way in which they can create different cadences when put together in different combinations. I did anticipate that a little bit with the fugue that opens *Lunch*, because the fugue is built in part on pieces of Stein.

CH: Let's talk specifically about religious iconography, which is never as simple as it seems, in your poems. In *Cocktails*, there are churches, crosses, the prodigal son, Mother Mary, an eerie "song of the undead" linked to Christ, and "a song of resurrection" set in winter that ends:

> in the town a church kept bare its cross: draped with the
>   purple tunic
> we knelt to the wood.   and this I tell you as gospel: the
>   sky shuddered
> a bolt shook our hearts on the horizon.   for what
>   seemed an eternity
> [for we knew eternity by the silence it brings] void:
>   then scudding rain

What attracts you to these images and themes?

DAP: Because an entire section of *Cocktails* is built on the Gospels, I realized that I was going to encounter certain problems, that is to say, certain stories that have to be incorporated. My problem as the poet was how to do it in a way that seems true and doesn't just seem "put on." Resurrection is something that seems impossible, difficult to conceive of in any type of rational mind. So, how does one write about resurrection?

CH: Are you pulled toward the iconography of the Gospels because of the tradition of poems in that area or because of your experience with religion and spirituality?

DAP: I realized one could project oneself into the Gospels just the way one could project oneself into a film scenario, for example. And it was a very transgressive act because so many times people try to write queerness out of the Bible.

There's something wonderful, too, about the show and glamour and drag of religion. I mean, if you go to John the Divine in New York, you might think, "If this place weren't a cathedral, it would be a nightclub." It's so beautiful and so astounding! They have that wonderful Keith Haring screen there. They have peacocks in the yard. It's *gay*—I mean *gay* in the old sense, and *gay* in every sense. A friend of mine sang countertenor with Chanticleer (he just retired this year), and they did an "all chant" concert a few years back at the Mission Dolores Basilica in San Francisco. They staged the whole thing in monks' robes by candlelight. I was sitting there listening to this beautiful music and watching the processionals. A friend turns to me in the middle of the concert and says, "You know, I never realized before how erotic the church is." And I said, "Thank God, I thought it was just me." [Laughs.]

CH: Robert Hass said your work "studiously avoids, though it is full of deaths, whatever is grave and noble in the hindsight of elegy." He's right—your elegies are haunting, moving, but outside the view of what might traditionally be seen as an elegy. How do you take on those poems?

DAP: Because they don't let anyone get away with being holy and lovely and elevated. I chalk that up to my own youth. Those poems [from *Tea*] were written with a kind of brashness that I don't know that I would have now, but I'm glad that there was something of value in them. For me, it really was a desire to both elegize and at the same time lay waste to the elegiac mode, which is a pretty heavy aspiration.

CH: Was avoiding sentimentality in writing the elegy imperative for you?

DAP: Yes, well, I feel that sentimentality was so done to death in the '70s. I feel that so many poets are trying to avoid the personal because they somehow wed it to the sentimental. I wanted to see if it was possible to be both personal and unsentimental. I think that there may be times where it doesn't quite work, to be perfectly honest, but there were a few moments in that book where it really did work and I was happy to bring back the "I."

I don't feel that you have to abandon subject in order to write an objective poem. You simply have to marry the subjectivity with objectivity. It's just a matter of striking the right balance.

CH: It always seems shortsighted when people refuse to write about themselves for fear of going down a sentimental road, because, of course, they have some control over this. Have poets conflated writing about the self with some sort of tacky confessionalism?

DAP: [Writing from the personal] takes a while to figure out how to do it in a way that works for you. My early mentor, someone who was a huge influence on me, David Bromige, has a poem in his book *Tiny Courts* [*in a World without Scales*] where he says, "and 'I' cannot mean 'me.'" I think that is not just wit—it's wisdom. There has to be some sense of distance so that you can work through the problems of the poem without wanting to labor over the self.

For the most part, you really can't be wedded to fact. What Keats says about negative capability, the willingness to dwell in doubt and uncertainty without the irritable reaching after fact and reason, that's not just an idea to me—that's a law. Different poets talk about it in different ways. It's Lorca's *duende* or [Jack] Spicer's Martians. There's some other part of the self, some irrational part of the self, that you have to allow to come in and do a good deal of the poem, because otherwise it does get terrible.

And Lord knows, I spent a long time writing bad poems. I did it as a practice because I wanted to figure out what made a poem bad. It was hard for me to set out to write a good poem and end up with a good poem, but it was pretty easy to set out to write a bad poem and end up with a bad poem. I did it for a couple of years. For me that was really valuable because I went down the road of the negative, *via negativa*, in order to find what my own poetics and what my own values were. I have my students often construct their own poetics, and it's difficult for them, but I give them the example of thinking about not so much what they're writing in favor of, but what they're writing against. Think of the real innovators—Rimbaud isn't trying to exalt poetry as a new god, he's really trying to smash the idols of the past. [Walt] Whitman, certainly, is striking out and trying to make a whole new thing that's in response to the horrible, constrained poems of his past. William Carlos Williams said "bad art is . . . that which does not serve in the continual service of cleansing the language of all fixations upon the dead, stinking dead, usages of the past." You have to be striking out into some new territory.

Of course, now everyone's trying to be new, and the result is a kind of homogeneity.

CH: A lot of poems in that vein really require the readers to project their own emotions onto that poem to find emotions anywhere. A lot of poems seem encased in a shell of irony—and what's inside, I wonder.

DAP: Think about [Wallace] Stevens, for example, because a lot of poets hold Stevens up as a god. I think that Stevens is a wonderful poet, but if there is something held in abeyance, which is the self, there is at least something else that substitutes; and sometimes it's at the level of the sonority and rhythm of the poem; sometimes it's at the level of play; sometimes it's at the level of image. But the poems always resolve themselves into a space in which you feel that you've been moved—that no matter what compositional technique he's foregrounding, there's a pulse underneath. There's a human being that the poem is referencing, if only obliquely, if only to say: This is about hiding from God and hiding from the personal.

I feel that way with Stein. The stakes are very high for her. When she creates these complex texts, she's also at the same time revealing so much about her own insecurities. She is putting into them, hiding in plain sight, references to her relationship with Alice Toklas. She's making a bold political move because she realizes that she's writing a kind of poetry that is not popular. So for her to write the kind of poem that she writes, at the time that she writes it, is really a kind of defiant act. It's in defiance of patriarchy. It's in defiance of the canon, of tradition, of Western culture.

CH: "This is not a book about AIDS," you begin in a preface to *Tea*, arguing that the disease doesn't hold dominion over the poems—

DAP: I hate when [works] are reduced to their subjects. Also, there's a way in which, for a while, AIDS was made precious by our culture . . . that is, once Americans finally got around to addressing it as an issue of humanity, which took a long time. Then, it was like an easy play at the heartstrings: *Oh*, AIDS, *so sad*—you know? I wanted to quickly sidestep that and say: "Look, if that's what you're after, this book ain't gonna be it." I don't want to be a part of that body. Please, leave me out of that little game.

CH: The reason I think it's interesting people are parsing things out as "AIDS literature" is that there's this immense range of work, from Paul Monette's revered books, to Thom Gunn's now legendary *The Man with Night Sweats*—

DAP: I think Thom [was] an amazing poet. I love his poems. I feel that I learn so much from reading his work. That said, I felt that *The Man with Night Sweats* was organized in such a way that it vectored toward a finale of death. That's been the queer storyline for so long: if you introduce a queer character in the first act, you have to kill him off by the third. That was actually written into the morals code in filmmaking: if there's a queer character, they have to suffer somehow. (Vito Russo did this wonderful necrology of how queer characters were killed off in film after film after film.)

Because I think about books as narratives—it's not just a collection of discrete poems, but an underlying story line that pushes you forward—I didn't want something that ended with dying. *Tea* really was a response to that. I put the dying at the beginning, and then it was about the phoenix rising from the ashes and saying: Now that we've experienced loss, how do we go on? How do we think about survival? How do we think about how that loss intersects with living? Proust says, "Such are the unenviable forms of survival," and that's what I use to open the book—to say that this is the real crisis: living, not dying. Dying is easy . . .

CH: And you've said that the price of survival is memory.

DAP: Sorry, not to say that dying is easy. From a *literary* standpoint it's easy.

CH: With writing about AIDS, there's a point where it gets sticky. How to set the great poems beside a lot of stuff that just doesn't seem to rise to the level of poetry? How do you critique those poems?

DAP: You're talking about the ones that are so much about the subject that they hold the subject like a Fabergé egg, and you can't touch the poem without breaking the egg? Well, you don't really talk about those poems. The people who write those poems needed to write them for whatever reason. Poetry isn't just an art form—it's also a place where people go. It's a confessional. It's a place of solace and comfort, and we can't ignore that. The history of poetry is filled with all sorts of poetry that was written for the wrong reasons. It's not just "AIDS literature." If you go back to the seventeenth century, there are plenty of bad elegies about people who drowned or who died in childbirth. With time, the bad poems disappear. These poems that don't hold up as great works of literature, they'll disappear too; but for now, people need to write them. That doesn't mean we have to read them, and it doesn't mean that if we do read them we have to say, "Oh, that was terrible." We just turn the page.

CH: Your own writing about the disease runs the gamut of tones: "no permanent fixture the flesh" and "greensick in our salad days! . . . we cellophaned. . . . afraid of the rash our craving would provoke." No easy task, I'm guessing. Does this come naturally, or do you consciously decide to write in varied tones?

DAP: I think I whistle through the graveyard. [Laughs.] If I feel that I've gone too far in one direction, I have to compensate by going in the other direction. I have really no sacred cows in the poem. Everything that is venerated is also undercut. I like to undercut my own authority because it's too boring to have all the answers, and I don't know how anyone could have all the answers. I might have come close to having all the questions.

CH: Your work is steeped in figurative language, especially metaphor—from a sort of searching ("a cloak an ache a thief in the night") to the declaration ("for I was a stone: washed in the stream. . . . I was cut clean . . .") to whole poems based on a figure, like the Minotaur poem in *Lunch* where you write, "myself am halfboy. . . . am beauty and the end of same: a hungry thing / hunts me also." I feel like metaphor, simile, analogy—the palette of figurative language—is felt so deeply that it serves as an idiom for you? [Pauses.] But you wrote in your introduction, "I don't understand metaphor."

DAP: Yes, and I'm not being coy. In some ways I actually don't understand metaphor. I'm so used to looking at the world through some set of lenses—whatever set of lenses happens to be available at the moment. I always find the similarities between things or I find some sort of connection. I think that's part of what makes a poet a poet, the fact that Pablo Neruda can look at an artichoke and see a warrior, the fact that Eliot can look at the fog and see a cat—and never name it as a cat, because then it's metonym, not metaphor. There are some people who naturally see the world that way and learn how to tap into it and make art out of it.

CH: Some poets can put on lenses to understand the world, but I feel that it's so much a part of your work that it's not a lens, but the very eye of you. That's just how you see, whereas other poets put on glasses.

DAP: Maybe it just feels put-on when they do it.

CH: Any thoughts on how to avoid that? It's almost an impossible question.

DAP: It is an impossible question because I feel that so much of poetry really is drag and that the put-on is really an essential part of it. Robert Duncan has this notion of the "enabling fiction"—the little story we tell ourselves in order to get ourselves to do what it is we do—and I think that poets have these enabling fictions. My enabling fiction is probably that I don't see any barrier between the language of the world and the world itself. It's probably not true—see, I even have to say "probably," because if I allow myself for a moment to stop believing that I believe that, then I'll have lost it, it'll have eluded me.

I'm interested in the way that in Chinese written characters the word itself embodies not just the thing but also the component parts that come to make the thing. I really believe that language is the way to call the world into being, that "in the beginning was the word and the word became flesh." If we have the word for something then we can make the thing out of it, and not the other way around. So when I compile words, I'm working in a kind of alchemical laboratory. I am really making the world out of language. I feel probably more of a connection to poets like Robert Duncan and Wallace

Stevens. For these poets, it really is a matter of going to the world and finding the word that you can hold up against the experience of the world and say, "These two things seem to match."

Almost as soon as you do that, you also become aware of all the other things that that word refers to, and you can't ever unlearn it, because each word casts a certain stain upon the next one. So you learn how they begin to fit together and create subtext within the text. I love to be at play in the field of language. Once a figure begins to emerge that is not at the forefront, but lying underneath the surface of the poem, I start to also pay attention to it—the way Michelangelo could see Moses in the rock, I can see the subject buried in the language.

CH: Here are some of my favorite lines from the *Cocktails* (from a poem called "[dogs and boys can treat you like trash.and dogs do love trash]"):

> he closes his eyes to your kisses.   he hisses.   a boy is a
>   putz
>
> with a sponge for a brain.   and a mop for a heart: he'll
>   soak up your love
> if you let him and leave you as dry as a cork.   he'll
>   punch out your guts

There's a limerick quality to some of this, a playfulness that is eerily at home with the violence of the poem. Your work walks this tightrope, in terms of being right down the line between two sides, two very opposite tones. Does that metaphor resonate for you in terms of this poem?

DAP: I like to think of it as a teeter-totter, but a tightrope works—except that I'm afraid of heights. [Laughs.] It's a delicate balance. I feel that the world really operates on a series of oppositions. My teacher David Bromige used to say that there has to be friction; if there's nothing to push against, you're not going anywhere, the wheels just spin. You really need to feel that the poem is built out of dueling forces: one that's pushing in one direction and one that's pulling in the other. The idea is to complicate the poem so that you really don't know any one moment how to feel.

CH: Here's a great example of that, a poem that sexualizes the Santa Claus–and–child image, showing a sort of utter authority and fearlessness:

> but what's the use of being pretty if I won't get better?
> bouncing me against your red woolies you whisper: *dear*
> *boy*.   unzip your enormous sack.   pull me quick into
>   winter

Do you see your poetry as fearless?

DAP: *I* get disturbed by that poem. But I don't know that I'd ever thought of my poetry in terms of fearlessness. I am by nature fairly fearless. Despite all of my weaknesses as a human being, there is deep down something rash and gutsy about me that just never quite—I can't tame it. I don't know what to do about it sometimes. But in poetry, at least, I'm not playing with explosives *per se*. I feel that the poem is the one safe place that you can go and try different things.

I had to write an essay on my poetics recently, and I utilized the metaphor of the body for the poem. I don't know that I'm the first person to think of it that way, but the poem is, for me, a body. I think that it's no accident that most poets first start writing poetry around the same age that they start masturbating, because it's a similar kind of impulse: you are at play and exploring this tool, which is language. You get a charge out of the things that you can do with it. For a while you can get that charge endlessly, and then you have to make the game a little bit more complex. The fantasy has to get a little bit newer, more original, different. The language, the rhythms, the structure have to get more complex or different somehow in order to keep you interested.

CH: It's fascinating that so many poets, gay men especially, use the body as a metaphor for poetry.

DAP: When we talk about someone's work, we talk about it as a body. When we read a book, we are "getting between the covers"; we are leafing through the sheets with that author. There is a power that language has over the body. Certainly when you feel moved, you feel it somatically. You feel it in your gut, in your liver, in your heart, in the tingle on the surface of your skin. Words are the only thing, aside from another body, that can actually arouse you—unless you're twelve and are aroused by just a gentle breeze. [Both laugh.] But as you get older, it's the one place you can go and still feel that something happens in the body.

CH: I often like to ask poets about influence and working in a tradition. In your work, there's [John] Berryman's "tragical playfulness" (Bin Ramke's words), there's Whitman's teasing out of the line, [Hart] Crane's cipher-like quality, [Frank] O'Hara's ardor for pop culture, and even a tilt of the hat to E. E. Cummings, I think, in lines of yours like, " . . . .dearest perdition, your sweet peach kisses lost" [from *Lunch*]—

DAP: —Yes, Cummings has that kind of archness. I like his stagy quality. I'll cop to Whitman and Crane as well, and O'Hara.

CH: Are you consciously aware of these influences, and does writing ever feel schizophrenic?

DAP: I'm not so aware of those influences. I remember my first writing teacher saying to me, "Well, I see a lot of D. H. Lawrence in here." I had been reading D. H. Lawrence that semester, but I didn't feel like I had anything in common with him. The people that I always worry that I'm copying are poets like James Dickey, Sylvia Plath, Amiri Baraka, Lawrence Ferlinghetti, and [T. S.] Eliot—the poets that I fell in love with so much when I was young that I felt like I was stealing from them. But no one ever sees those influences anymore, so I guess I've grown or developed my own set of concerns.

I can tell you all of the first poetry books that I owned in order of my owning them. They were: *The Black Poets* anthology by Dudley Randall; *Wasteland and Other Poems* by Eliot; *The Cricket Sings*, a translation of [Federico García] Lorca by Will Kirkland; Plath's *Ariel*; *Coney Island of the Mind* by Ferlinghetti; *Howl and Other Poems* by [Allen] Ginsberg; *Cotton Candy on a Rainy Day* by Nikki Giovanni—

CH: How do you remember that?

DAP: I have that kind of memory.

CH: It's funny, you and I have talked about the obsessive-compulsive quality of gay men, and there's a good example of it. I think I also see that in your work, in the fact that every poem has a piece of a previous poem in it, not always literally, but there's a sense of continuation throughout your books.

DAP: I like to bury things in my poems. There'll be buried puns and allusions and references to other works, other poets. There's even a lot of hidden pop culture in *Cocktails*. For example, if you look for them, you can find the names of all of the characters in Nina Simone's song "Four Women," but you wouldn't notice them unless you were looking for them.

CH: Does that sensibility become a form, in a sense, giving you a framework within which to write?

DAP: Well, I often tell my students to follow your natural obsessions, because that's where you'll find your style and your subject, the particular tics that are your own. For me, that's a kind of practice.

I also like to make word lists, and in fact a lot of my poems are lists. I think that's one of the reasons that I love David Trinidad's work, because he has poems that are made up of lists. (Gertrude Stein said that poems are really just lists of nouns.) I have this kind of nesting that I do where, before I get too far into the poem, I start to list all of the things that could go into it. I don't necessarily know the subject, but I know the general place that I'm writing towards for that particular poem. So, I list things around the bottom and sides of the page and cross them off as I use them. They can be words, phrases, ideas, or images. Assemblage is really a good way of thinking about it: the poem as made thing. It's why I like Marianne Moore so much, because she's like a bird: she finds the shiny little object, and she weaves it into the nest somehow. Spencer Short is also a poet who does that, and he describes it that way. Brenda Hillman was the first poet I met who talked about nesting, and I immediately saw that it was an apt description of my practice.

CH: That reminds me of the fugue in the first and second books. What attracts you to that form? Does it allow the poet to say something about memory, perhaps?

DAP: Before I was even attracted to poetry, I was attracted to the fugue as a device. It could be the *Grosse Fugue* of Beethoven. Or it could be that wonderful moment in *A Little Night Music* by Stephen Sondheim where he's got three separate songs sung by three separate characters—one is "Now," one is "Later," and one is "Soon"—and then they all merge into one song. I feel that's really the central organizing principle in my mind: that things will recur at odd moments, and they begin to echo off of one another. Philip Guston and René Magritte both do this in their paintings, so I'm not alone.

I wanted to do a third fugue in *Cocktails*, but then I thought that it's going to be expected, so I give a coda and a discography. Because I think of the three books as together constituting a kind of *Divine Comedy*, with *Tea* being the underworld because it's full of buried bodies, and *Lunch* as a kind of *Purgatorio*, that thing that you want to get through quickly. *Cocktails* is my *Paradiso*. So when I get to the discography, the lines resolve themselves into tercets, and I actually end on the word "star" to make a little homage to Dante. It's also an homage to the disco singer Sylvester, because that was the title of one of his songs: it's his song that ends the discography. (See how "disco" is buried in the title?)

CH: Let's end by looking at a beginning: how you came to complete your first book. You write in *Tea* that you were compelled to write again after a year of grieving and that you found you were unable to contain your lines, that they pushed past the margins. Did you find that flipping the notebook sideways freed you imaginatively as well, not just structurally?

DAP: Yes, I think it did free me up imaginatively. From the earliest time in which we begin to write, we're instructed to leave that margin. For me that imperative was absolutely damaging and constricting. I noticed it first when I was teaching poetry writing at Sonoma State, before I went off to do my MFA. My students' poems always seemed to try to resolve themselves before they reached the bottom of the page. As interesting as the poem was, it would seem as though, "oops, the page is running out." And the lines would want to resolve themselves about two inches from the edge of the page. I felt like it was the page that was the problem. I was always instructing my students to write on different sizes of paper than the sizes they would normally write on, to use different implements, to slow down when they would want to speed up, to not allow themselves to erase, all sorts of things like that. It was slightly later—you know, "physician, heal thyself"—than the moment at which I had written that prescription for others, that I began to see that it could be of use for myself.

CH: Are the lessons learned from that experience still echoing in your work today?

DAP: I'm keenly aware of edge in many senses, and boundaries, and solutions to those boundaries. Caroline Knox just sent me this poem [holds up a Möbius strip with a poem written on it]. It has no boundary, no edge: a poem in an endless circle. That's another way of breaking through the barrier. It makes me want to write; that's the greatest compliment that you can pay to someone else's work: it makes me want to write.

D. A. POWELL

[dogs and boys can treat you like trash. and dogs do love trash]

dogs and boys can treat you like trash. and dogs do love trash
to nuzzle their muzzles. they slather with tongues that smell like their nuts

but the boys are fickle when they lick you. they stick you with twigs
and roll you over like roaches. then off with another: those sluts

with their asses so tight you couldn't get them to budge for a turd
so unlike the dogs: who will turn in a circle showing & showing their butts

a dog on a leash: a friend in the world. he'll crawl into bed on all fours
and curl up at your toes. he'll give you his nose. he'll slobber on cuts

a dog is not fragile; he's fixed. but a boy: cannot give you his love
he closes his eyes to your kisses. he hisses. a boy is a putz

with a sponge for a brain. and a mop for a heart: he'll soak up your love
if you let him and leave you as dry as a cork. he'll punch out your guts

when a boy goes away: to another boy's arms. what else can you do
but lie down with the dogs. with the hounds with the curs. with the mutts

[when you touch down upon this earth.
little reindeers]

when you touch down upon this earth. little reindeers
hoofing murderously at the gray slate roof: I lie beneath
dearest father xmas: will you bring me another 17 years

you gave me my first tin star and my first tin wreath
warm socks tangerines and a sloppy midnight kiss
I left you tollhouse cookies. you left me bloody briefs

lipodystrophy neurosthesia neutropenia mild psychosis
increased liver enzymes increased bilirubin and a sweater
don't get me wrong: I like the sweater. though it itches

but what's the use of being pretty if I won't get better?
bouncing me against your red woolies you whisper: *dear
boy*: unzip your enormous sack. pull me quick into winter

CHRISTOPHER HENNESSY

Sick Room

My love, my Lethe (an ebb has begun)—
        the terror of being alone
        is replaced by my fingers' arthritic
        worrying of your braided bones:
                to ease the caving ribs away.

Fever is hostage for you,
        my dear wound, my truce.

My spit is a tasteless poultice
        and my breath is
        leaves of mint on your chest.

I am ridden, I
        am prone, here.
        I am the ever-present room,
        curtained contagion.

An original, iron heat
        snakes through you,
        and I can only press it deeper—invisible
        waves—into the scored creases
                I've left.

Cold press, a cloth,
        brittle ice in a bowl,
                an orphaned promise:

If I sleep, if I leave
        you . . . if I melt
                like the pearled ice,

then I become
        the sick room,
                the origin.

" Here she is: girl in a golden city, still seeing the world with Waynesboro eyes. Though how else would A. J. Wojak ever view the world? If not through her own eyes, then whose? "

MARY BETH CASCHETTA

Hands of God

HELENA FRANKEL HAS the squarest teeth A. J. Wojak has ever seen. It strikes her as odd to realize this now of all times, well into their third mid-Atlantic hour of flight to a place neither has been before. In fact, neither has been anywhere before, and so Helena has begun to speak of Italy in absolute terms: "Finally somewhere!" Helena is wonderful that way. In fact, just moments before getting lost in her best friend's teeth, A. J. was thinking about how Helena is the most beautiful girl in all of Waynesboro, Pennsylvania—place of their birth, and exactly *nowhere*—and also how weird it is that Helena is A. J.'s best friend. At the same time, in the back of A. J.'s mind, she has started to realize that she is growing bored with her. The thought is nearly unthinkable, and so A. J. revises: She is growing bored with Helena's break-up saga, which has been the topic of conversation nonstop since boarding the plane at five this morning.

Neither here nor there, A. J. thinks wistfully, looking out at clouds.

She and Helena have saved money two years for this trip, arranged the timing carefully, sorting out A. J.'s high school vacation and Helena's holiday work schedule. The real problem is that A. J. is no longer stoned, which means she is irritated, which means she should remedy the situation by suggesting a trip to the bathroom, which she will do as soon as she can get a word in edgewise. In the meantime, her slow buzzing mind has landed on bicuspids. Helena's are bone white, perfectly rounded for the tearing of flesh, though she is strictly vegetarian, which A. J. admires. Also, because of a slight speech impediment, even the hardest consonants slipping from Helena's lips are slightly wet and smooth. It's a pleasant sound, Helena talking, if you can loosen your mind around the content. Two days before the trip, Helena discovered her boyfriend, Gordon Johnson, a foreman at the P&G, in bed with someone else.

"Not just someone," Helena says, reviewing the facts. "But two someones! I mean, A. J., Gordy was in bed with *a couple*—a girl *and* her husband."

She is clutching the love note she found stuffed in Gordy's wallet, which almost caused her to cancel the trip, except that Easter was the only week that wouldn't affect her paycheck. Procter & Gamble is closed Holy Thursday, Good Friday, and the following Monday.

There is a world, A. J. tells herself, *a wide, wide world.*

"I mean, a threesome, A. J.!" Helena says. "A married couple with a baby and everything!"

Helena is wearing jeans that pinch her boyish hips and angle way out at her ankle. There's a rip in her turtleneck sweater, which is cream-colored and nearly matches her skin. A. J. marvels that Helena's father let her out of the house that way. When she thinks of her own father—a guy who drives a school bus, was unanimously elected to town council, and makes a mean gin martini—her mind goes blank. Her body produces a numb floating sensation, as if she's stoned, as if the very thought of his existence wipes hers out entirely. A. J.'s father let her travel mostly because of Helena, about whom he maintains a positive opinion: *People can say what they will about Kikes, but Helena Frankel is good people, a darn pretty little thing.*

Helena is Jewish, but no one in Waynesboro seems to mind—no one treats her like it. Besides, the Frankels have been part of the town since the beginning; they own a drug store on East Main.

Now, she is grimacing, twisting her lips strangely and wiping away tears, so that A. J. has to squint to detect the senior voted most likely to succeed, class of '72.

Helena lowers her voice. "He'd go there for dinner, and after the kid was in bed, they lit a fire in the fireplace and the three of them had major sex—all together at the same time—in the living room. He told me that, A. J."

A. J. is impressed with the idea that a regular guy like Gordy Johnson might not be so regular. A. J. can practically close her eyes and see Gordy in bed, his tall angular body, his weird yellow hair, huffing and puffing for the pleasure of some bored faceless housewife and her not-so-bored faceless husband. Accidentally for a minute, she imagines Helena there, too, naked on the rug next to Gordy *and* the married couple. She opens her eyes and stares at a woman sleeping across the aisle, realizing the picture is wrong. *Too many people.*

In her backpack, she has some marijuana, rolled and ready to go, which they will smoke if Helena ever stops talking about Gordy's perversions.

"But did Gordy actually *have sex* with the guy?" A. J. asks. "I mean did he say that he did?"

Helena pulls back a handful of frizzy red hair and tucks it in her collar. "That's what I've been trying to tell you, A. J. The guy'd been in Vietnam, and Gordy felt guilty because he couldn't go on account of all that mental stuff from his past. The war was like a connection Gordy had with this guy. They were both messed up about it—the guy because he went, and Gordy because he couldn't go."

"Oh," A. J. says.

It is 1973, she reminds herself, the year of her graduation. In two short months, she'll be working at the P&G like everyone else, and maybe then she'll be the one with the story to tell.

"I'd be messed up, too," A. J. says, "if I had to go to Vietnam."

Helena bites down hard on an airline coffee cup. "Stupid fuck-ing war."

It would be nice if Helena would name a few names: Gordy Johnson's faceless couple, to be exact. But she decides not to press the point, since Helena can be touchy, and they've got a solid week ahead of them in Florence, Venice, Rome. Anyway, it's easy enough in a small town to find out who someone like Gordy is fucking. To remind herself that everything's different now that they've left Pennsylvania, A. J. occupies her mind with thoughts of ancient ruins, pungent night clubs, not-quite-sanitary youth hostels.

"Gordon said having that guy's dick inside him brought him back to life," Helena whispers.

"Well, free love," A. J. says sympathetically, imagining Gordy's ass in the air, not quite sure whether she's in favor or against. Either way, it sounds poetic.

Helena sighs. "Man, you can say that again."

A. J. waves her beaded bag of joints in the air. "Bathroom?"

Helena nods, getting up slowly and making her way toward a slim aisle of tiny bathrooms at the back of the plane. She disturbs not one but two sleeping women with infants in their arms, knocking her hip into the seats so the women look up, surprised, and clutch their babies tighter. A. J. follows behind, smiling apologetically, knowing that Helena is merely trying to exact revenge against the half of a couple that's breaking her heart. At the back of the cabin, Helena nods toward a stewardess in a blue jersey who saunters down the opposite aisle. "Wait till she passes. I'll leave it unlatched."

As if on cue, the stewardess turns and looks at A. J., raising an eyebrow like a thinly plucked question mark. A. J. waves innocently, hesitating slightly before ducking inside and locking the door.

"Coast is clear," she says, announcing her success.

In the cramped space above the sink, A. J. produces a joint, lighting it quickly and taking two long, deep drags, which burn her lungs and feel good. She eventually lets the smoke waft out and the sweet tingling sensation wade in. Against her closed eyelids is an imprint of weird Gordy Johnson with his tongue in some man's mouth.

Waiting her turn, Helena muses, "When we get to Italy, let's fuck guys like crazy."

A. J. nods, holding out the joint for Helena's remarkable mouth, which is thin at the corner and wide toward the middle, a spoon. Gracefully, the pink lips touch each other, as Helena leans in for a hit of A. J.'s reefer.

AFTER DROPPING OFF their bags and smoking a joint with some Italians at a hostel next to the Pitti Palace, Helena grabs A. J.'s hand and they start off toward the old center. A. J. concentrates on a tourist's map of the ancient city. At first sight, Florence is disappointing—smallish and blunt, yellowy-gold, the color of a stubbed-out cigarette. *Nicotine stain*, A. J. thinks, disappointed that there's never any way of anticipating the imperfections of a place. Perhaps the future will merely be a series of letdowns, proving to A. J. that the only real location is the mind. She bites her nails and rustles the map. *What if the destination always mirrors its exact point of departure?* This notion freaks her out. *What if it's me?* Here she is: girl in a golden city, still seeing the world with Waynesboro eyes. Though how else would A. J. Wojak ever view the world? If not through her own eyes, then whose?

"Come on, A. J.," Helena says, grabbing the map where it folds. "We don't need this thing." Helena's breath is a peppermint airplane candy. "Give it up." She laughs. She threads her arm through A. J.'s and pulls her along. "I can't stand how beautiful this place is!"

A. J. appreciates Helena's point: Florence is far better than anything they've ever seen. Still, the difference between here and there is small and disturbing. *What if it's essentially the same wherever you are?* she thinks, longing to be lifted up and out of her own tedious mind, her lumpy, too-big body. As Helena weaves them around two old women selling trinkets on a long arching bridge, she considers sharing the realization that the difference between being alive and being dead, between being herself and not herself, is very, very small. *Infinitesimal*, she'd like to say aloud.

The thought gives her a chill.

Don't go over-thinking the experience, Helena would say. She once explained how Gordy had over-thought peas, an exercise that landed him in the County Hospital. For months, all he could do was talk about peas: their size, their shape, the different colors they came in. He became obsessed with the incredible beauty of such a small vegetable; when you thought about peas long enough, he'd claimed, you could no longer imagine anything more powerful.

A. J. makes a mental note, *Steer clear of peas.*

"God," Helena giggles, still stoned. "I think I'm going to explode. I mean, look at that, will you?" She points to the first of many David's they will see during the week.

A. J. snaps a photo of the statue and begins to relax a little, letting Helena's enthusiasm carry her forward. Her fingers are laced loosely in Helena's hands; the cool temperature of her skin is comforting.

When they arrive at the next place, Helena throws her arms around A. J.'s hips. "I want my life to be like this always," she says. "You and me and Florence forever."

In Italy, it is still early morning; they have an entire day for sightseeing ahead.

They stop and roll a joint, which A. J. lights under the *Rape of the Sabine Women.*

Above their heads, a great bell is ringing from the heart of the city.

THE BEAUTIFUL BOY selling his art outside the Uffizi is muscled in a modest way. A. J. has passed by his blanket a dozen times, noticing that he hasn't sold a single drawing all afternoon.

"You want to buy one?" he finally says.

A. J. is by herself because Helena has run off with a high-school basketball star from the Midwest, a guy who was sitting on the street, drinking wine, tall and lanky. Helena introduced herself. His name was Roger. He was on a class trip but could steal away if she wanted to see the Duomo.

Now A. J. is stoned, wandering the city alone. It is early evening. "This one. The heart-shaped pebble."

The beautiful boy laughs: "It's a clove of garlic."

"Oh," A. J. cocks her head. "How much?"

His T-shirt ripples. "More than you've got."

A. J. sniffs the breeze: "You don't know that."

"Maybe," he smiles. "Where's your friend? The one with the hair?"

A. J. likes that he's noticed them. "She went off with someone she just met."

The boy frowns. "What's the matter, you don't approve of love?"

"Love?" A. J. is hard-pressed to apply the word to Helena and Roger-from-Cleveland fucking against some ancient crucifix. "More like revenge."

The boy carefully wraps his charcoals up in a rag. "This is Florence. Magical things happen."

A. J. is doubtful.

He puts his sketches carefully inside a giant envelope, hesitating before picking up the garlic. "What's your name?" he asks.

"Alice-James."

"You Americans have weird names." He sticks out his hand. "*Yo soy Pedro de Cuba.*"

WHILE A. J. IS KISSING Pedro from Cuba, an image of her baby brother floats up. She clasps the back of Pedro's neck for more pressure and tries to settle into the pillow, wanting his mouth to blot hers out. *Feel it*, she tells herself, the numbness somehow reminding her of the floaty, lifeless feeling of growing up in Pennsylvania. Pedro lifts her shirt and kisses her breasts. She works her hand down his naked back and wonders if she should enter him, where he is not quite wet, but moist—sweaty. This is what keeps a man feeling alive, according to Gordy. A picture of Helena laughing floats up, mercifully relieving her, but doesn't stay. Her baby brother leans a head on her shoulder and coos like a little bird. She can recall the squeak of his talcomy skin, his tiny erections, which sometimes she touched when no one was looking. Then something else, something that frightens her. She can hear someone crying; her father, this time, with his head on her breast, or maybe the sound comes from her. Pedro sucks her nipples, as if she is a musical instrument on the verge of emitting some soft, sweet sound of pleasure. She concentrates instead on maneuvering into an arch to press her finger into his ass.

"Not so fast," Pedro whispers. "Take it easy."

A. J. reminds herself that she is lying naked on a cot in Pedro's studio in Florence. She hears the sounds from Via Dante Alighieri below; they are very near the Duomo. On their walk to dinner, Pedro had carefully pointed out the site of the great poet's restored medieval home. At the restaurant that seemed like someone's home, he quoted a few lines from the *Inferno* in Italian in a way that seemed only slightly rehearsed. On the walk back to his studio, they had turned corner after corner into plaza after plaza of tourists scouting out ice cream, pigeons flapping their wings. The strange world filled A. J. up like a song. She felt alive to be walking in Florence with a stranger, Pedro, who laughed and pointed out sights and called her *Niña*.

Now, lying with Pedro, she lights a joint for him and one for herself. This is an offering of love——*well, maybe not love*, she thinks, *but something*—because he saved her, because he knows her, because this is her very first time. One joint entirely for him.

"I've never been high before," Pedro says, smiling. "I like it."

"I've never been fucked before." A. J. laughs.

Pedro's features soften. "This is an honor, then."

For a moment, A. J. feels like crying. Pedro puts the marijuana on the windowsill, kissing her gently, placing himself between her legs and entering slowly, touching a chord, something like pain but also like lightness. It is sad suddenly to be so human, A. J. thinks—so merely human. When she opens her eyes, the room swirls. What she recalls is another room from another time. Perhaps this is the essential experience of sex, she thinks; you remember places from your past, or perhaps they are places from your future. She cannot tell. She doesn't know if her eyes are open or closed, or suddenly who it is, sweaty and gasping, on top of her. She grips the body and pulls it close, hoping for—if nothing else—an end. When finally it is over and Pedro stops moving, breathing heavily into her neck, sliding slowly out of her body, they lie still. They share a joint.

Pedro says, "You are no virgin, *mi amor*."

A. J. covers her body with the stale blanket; her breasts seem to spill over onto the bed, her stomach looks fat, her feet too big. She is doughy and pale, enormous in the dark room with the dark man, a stranger, who is about to fall asleep, to leave her there alone.

"That was my first time," A. J. says quietly, insistently.

Tears make the room a blur, and she sees now that her life depends on certain half-truths, on certain difficult propositions. Pedro takes her hand, kissing the knuckles. "Don't listen to me, *Niña*. Really. Pedro is foolish."

When they fall asleep, he squeezes his shoulders into the mattress, pinning her slightly against the wall.

IN THE MORNING, as planned, A. J. rushes to meet Helena at the Piazza Santa Croce. Jet-lagged and late from oversleeping, A. J. is almost glad that this time it will be Helena who gets there first, waiting on her for a change. Helena is too beautiful for her own good, A. J. decides anyway, her teeth are too white, and she's a total liar, *You and me and Florence forever*. Hurrying along, A. J. breaks into a sweat and has to stop to catch her breath. *Too much smoking*, she thinks. Near the Bapistry, the strangest feeling overtakes her, a kind of dizzy sensation that someone is standing on top of the Campanile, 276 feet above her head. Someone is pointing a rifle at her, someone slowly pulling her into the crosshair view and taking aim. She walks more quickly, heads over to the Ponte Vecchio, where the sweet-faced Italians will soon be setting up shop. *Love thy brother,* she thinks, sweating, sick to her stomach. Tucking her shoulders up to her ears, she shoves her hands deep in her pockets, looking for a place in the famous city to get a cup of coffee. *The past doesn't matter*, A. J. tells herself. *It's the future that counts.*

Outside the cathedral, Helena grills A. J. about Pedro. "Did it hurt?" she wants to know. "Did you like it? The first time always hurts."

It didn't hurt.

"That's weird. It's supposed to hurt the first time." Helena lights a regular cigarette and sits on the step, pulling A. J. down beside her. They are both wearing the same clothes as yesterday, the same clothes they had on in Waynesboro, which now seems like a million miles away. A. J. sits. In her back pocket is the charcoal drawing folded in half along with the fifty lire she stole from Pedro, who was still asleep when she slipped out of his apartment.

"What about you?" A. J. says sullenly. Maybe in the end, she'll escape Waynesboro, too, and travel the world, making everyone she knows part of her past. "How was Roger?"

Helena frowns and pulls the lit cigarette between her lips. "Okay, I guess. Well, actually, Roger was kind of gay. Nothing happened. I went back to the hostel."

Although Pedro was sweet, A. J. would give anything to have spent the night with Helena. She could have avoided the smell of his body, his small uncomfortable cot, the question he left swirling inside her brain.

"Gay?" Her head is pounding. "Not another one?"

Helena laughs and sticks out her tongue. "Who asked you?" She jumps up then, and skips up the steps to the cathedral.

Straining to her feet, A. J.'s limbs feel made of stone: "Wait for me." *Miraculous Helena bouncing back*, she thinks, trailing behind. Not a hundred brushes with imperfect love will ever weigh her down.

INSIDE SANTE CROCE, it smells of moldy devotion. The great cathedral is dimly lit and packed with the old women praying. At the holy water fountain, under the enormous vaulted ceiling, Helena stands close behind A. J. She can feel heat radiating off her body and smell the soapy smell of her flesh. Perhaps this is how close Helena gets to two-timing Gordy, and poor, gay Roger from Cleveland, Ohio.

A. J. looks across the row of pews, longer than a football field, down a separate hallway, where there are statues and paintings as far as the eye can see, elaborate ceramics, stations of the cross. At one popular corner, you can put a coin in a slot to light up the Lord, a famous twelfth-century carving. *A mall for the Savior*, A. J. thinks. Through the dark they make their way past the monuments of Michelangelo, Galileo, Machiavelli.

"I need a joint," she says.

"You know what day it is, don't you?"

A. J. thinks it over. "The second day of you and me and Florence?"

"Good Friday," Helena corrects. "The day the Jews killed Jesus. My people, your Lord. I hope you're not still mad about that."

A. J.'s laugh breaks the silence, causing a few kneeling women to look up from their prayers. She covers her mouth and speaks in a muffled tone. "All the more reason I need to smoke."

Helena drags her to the sacristy to light a candle. "Come on," she whispers, pulling A. J. to her knees. "Save our souls."

A. J. rolls her eyes.

"Say a prayer, A. J. You're Catholic. You know, *Forgive me father* and all that jazz."

"I don't know the words."

They settle on their knees before Jesus, who is nailed to his cross. His pinched, mournful face makes A. J. think that maybe he did something to deserve such a fate. She considers the bind he is in. People don't just go around getting their wounds doused with vinegar for nothing. Son of God, or not, he might have done better to keep his mouth shut. But this is not the point, she remembers. Someone had to die for someone. A. J. herself is nearly free—nearly eighteen—nearly gone. Her brother and sister will be left behind to talk about how she got out. *Better them than me left behind*, she thinks, feeling guilty for not ever having saved anyone, maybe not even herself.

Now, Helena leans forward, so A. J. can smell her sweet smoky breath. She opens her mouth as if she's about to insist that A. J. say a prayer for her but instead presses her lips cautiously to A. J.'s mouth. They are warm and dry, her lips, accommodating. A. J. pulls back, but Helena kisses again, tongue lingering lightly on A. J.'s teeth.

"I always wondered." Helena smiles, shrugging. "It's kind of nice."

A. J. stares at the sad, birdlike face of Jesus, who stares back at her. She blushes and clears her throat, feeling ridiculous.

"Oh, don't be stupid, will you? It's no big deal." Helena jabs her with a good-natured elbow. "Meet me outside. Okay? I'm starving to death already."

An organ begins to play, the notes jumbled.

A. J. listens, unable to think up a single thought.

AS SHE STEPS out of San Croce, the light strikes A. J.'s face as if it were fire. The yellow-gold is so bright that she has to squint at the sun and the warmth, thankful to be alive, she reminds herself. Helena is waiting for her on the bottom step, waving and grinning. She is saying something loudly—perhaps A. J.'s name—when a magical little crowd of children appears out of nowhere, separating them, rushing toward A. J., who smiles at first, happy to see their grubby little faces, their tight balled-up fists, raised toward Heaven in exultation. *Who are they?* A. J. wonders, as they rush in, poking and prodding, fingers digging into her ribs and pockets. This close, she can't tell whether they are children or tiny dirty women. They stand as tall as her waist and smell of rotten lettuce, hair matted and tangled, clothes made of rags. They squawk like birds, whistle, or smack the air, drawing A. J.'s eye first to the ground, then the sky; to the right and left, until A. J. is dizzy. One of them kisses her elbow; another throws herself at A. J.'s feet, pecking her ankles with biting little lips, as if for mercy. Their human stench is suffocating, their mesmerizing press surprisingly warm and forceful. They seek out A. J.'s softest places.

Suddenly, they are touching A. J. everywhere, bruising her skin like an old piece of fruit. At last, the disheveled creatures knock her to the ground, covering her completely like clouds over sun. Lying prone on the stone steps, A. J. smiles. The hands press in, as if searching for her soul. *Not there*, she thinks, relieved to know the truth at last. She will start over, pick herself up and begin anew, this time from scratch with no past at all. Through the crowd, she hears Helena call out her name. In the future she will be the kind of person who knows whether these terrible children mean to love her, or mean her harm, with their kisses and their small hands of God.

Glose

> Blood's risks, its hollows, its flames
> Exchanged for the pull of that song
> Bone-colored road, bone-colored sky
> Through the white days of the storm
>
> —Claire Malroux, "Storm"

Once out of the grip of desire,
or, if you prefer, its embrace,
free to do nothing more than admire
the sculptural planes of a face
(are you gay, straight or bi, are you *queer*?)
you still tell your old chaplet of names
which were numinous once, you replace
them with adjectives : witty, severe,
trilingual ; abstracting blood's claims,
blood's risks, its hollows, its flames.

No craving, no yearning, no doubt,
no repulsion that follows release,
no presence you can't do without,
no absence an hour can't erase :
the conviction no reason could rout
of being essentially wrong
is dispelled. What feels oddly like peace
now fills space you had blathered about
where the nights were too short or too long,
exhanged for the pull of that song.

But peace requires more than one creature
released from the habit of craving
on a planet that's mortgaged its future

to the lot who are plotting and raving.
There are rifts which no surgeon can suture
overhead, in the street, undersea.
The bleak plain from which you are waving,
mapped by no wise, benevolent teacher
is not a delight to the eye :
bone-colored road, bone-colored sky.

You know that the weather has changed,
yet do not know what to expect,
with relevant figures expunged
and predictions at best incorrect.
Who knows on what line you'll be ranged
and who, in what cause, you will harm?
What cabal or junta or sect
has doctored the headlines, arranged
for perpetual cries of alarm
through the white days of the storm?

Dialogue 21 / The reunion

On the last night before the reunion it rained/The cars pulled over
    to submit to it

The awnings The pavements The subway walls streaming/The
    lightning crossing the river's bed

Across from the lights of the city the thunder/playing the drum of
    the old palisades

The trees rooted in rock there The leaves/ducking and drinking the
    torrent Still green

In the early morning you could smell clarity/In the late morning
    you could smell smoke

Smoke of the apex Smoke of the windows/for viewing the archipel-
    ago from the sky

Smoke of the lost citizens of the empire/Their machines Their
    clothes Their wedding rings

Smoke of steel Smoke of fuel Smoke of glass and plastic/Smoke of
    the last words they found to say

Smoke of the planned delirium of hatred/Smoke of the planned
    delirium of fear

Smoke of the maimed messengers/from an unpronounceable place
    far away

Too far to hear before the reunion/But that morning plain enough
    I live

In the valley of the shadow of death/Let's live there together just for
    today

Dialogue 55 / To be continued

Once upon a time there was or there was not/a woman who stirred
and opened her eyes
On a world that did not include her enslavement/A world that did
not consist of this
Who woke in her ordinary nakedness/Who looked on her nakedness without shame
Her nakedness without mutilation/Her feet Her clitoris Her
unbound hair

Did you see her Undivided unsold daughter/Would you recognize
her if you saw her again
What was she called Do you remember/her way of walking The
words she said
Who closed her eyes in the darkness pressed/to the land to which
she belonged with the others
A woman whose tongue made council and pleasure/A woman who
was free

HOLLY IGLESIAS

Conceptual Art

An act of recovery, they say in curatorial tones, archiving the mundane, rooting through the baggage of inmates deposited long ago for safe-keeping, anonymity the new caché, a hunger for narrative free of consequence. Within a small strapped case, the single shirt, carefully starched, his winter drawers and the geography text once memorized to win a ribbon that Mother tacked to the parlor wall, boasting of her genius boy. Before he began drooling in church, tweezing the hairs from his forearm, singing to himself as he walked to the foundry after a breakfast of oats and beans and splashing his cheeks with her cologne. Before he began seeing things that weren't there and begged her for stories in Polish to soothe his fears, his grief for uncles buried in an old world and the clumsy name no one in town could pronounce. He lived out the balance of his days in gray pants and black shoes, took meals at six, twelve and six and dug graves when told to. His single pleasure, if you dare call it that, the school book, a quiet, solid thing upon his lap each afternoon, his fingers as smooth as the pages, patting it, stroking it, to calm the seas roiling between its covers.

"

'Yeah, whatever,' Jane says, stubbing out her cigarette on the bottom of her left patent leather Mary Jane. She goes immediately for another one, from a packet concealed in her pinafore. 'All I know is, I'm a forty-seven-year-old woman trapped in the body of an eleven-year-old girl. This is my sexual prime, for God's sake!'

"

JOHN ROWELL

Elementary Education

T'S THE LAST DAY of school, and my first graders are lining up to say good-bye to me. They do so with forlorn little faces, unenthusiastic handshakes. I take this as a compliment, a sure sign that they like me and that they'll miss me during the summer, though I fear there's another meaning behind their sorrow, too: they know I'm not coming back. These days, even six-year-olds are privy to a rumor mill.

Barely before the last child is out the door, I see Clara Griswold's long, spooky shadow slanting in the hallway; she is hovering about, witch-like, waiting to summon me to her office for the official firing. She pokes her prim, sour face around the doorway; if I hadn't known she was there already, I might have jumped out of my seat at the sight of her. If Clara Griswold hadn't founded a private school in the metropolis of Upper Reach, Massachusetts, (north of Boston, and a stone's throw, appropriately, from the town most famous for burning witches and heretics) she certainly would have had a lucrative career in horror movies.

"May I see you in my office please, Mr. Yardley?" she intones.

(Do I have a choice?)

She smiles at me from across her desk—the confident warmth of an executioner.

"Mr. Yardley, I'm sure you remember my saying back in September that your appointment here at the Griswold School was to be on a temporary basis, a trial."

(A trial. That's Salem language—circa 1695.)

". . . that we would give it the length of the school year, and then we would see how we did."

"Well, you've done just fine, Miss Griswold," I say, politely.

"I wasn't speaking of myself," she says, losing the smile. "Your teaching methods, Mr. Yardley, are . . . well, they're creative and colorful, certainly they are that. However, here at the Griswold School, we value the basics, the elementals of a child's education."

"I feel my students were quite happy with me," I say.

She pauses and purses her lips. She folds her bony, veiny hands in front of her on the desk. Maybe she's not a witch at all, maybe she's a witch-hunter: Governor Danforth in spinster drag.

"Yes, no argument there. I would say, in fact, perhaps *too* happy. I would also say, as a rule, that there seemed to be quite a lot of playing going on, more than actual learning, in your classroom. Particularly in the last few months. Have you been feeling all right, Mr. Yardley? Lately, I mean?"

She's referring to an unfortunate spell I had six weeks ago, when out of a combination of boredom, sleeplessness, and anxiety, I began talking to myself in front of the children. It only lasted about three or four minutes, just enough to really rivet them. In fact, they were transfixed; I might also add, immodestly, that they applauded me as soon as I snapped out of it. They seemed to view it as just another performance; throughout the year, I had been acting out fairy-tale characters and heroes from tall tales for them on a daily basis. They had become quite discerning where performance art was concerned, and I took it as high praise that they gave me an ovation for this particular episode, in which, I now know because they told me, I was hallucinating out loud an impromptu break-up I seem to have thought I was having with Richard Gere, whom, I also seem to have thought, I was having an affair with. Six-year-olds, let it be known, are smart in the ways of love.

"The children enjoyed it when I acted out characters," I say, though I know this doesn't sound convincing.

She smiles. She knows she has won.

"Well, I believe in tried and true methods for teaching children," she says. "For instance, to my way of thinking, there is no better way to teach children to read than with the good old Sally, Dick, and Jane readers. I firmly believe in them."

"Sally, Dick, and Jane?" I say, feeling as though I've been transported back to my own first grade years, thirty years ago. Yes, yes, that's it! Witches have the power to conjure magic; she's cast a spell and sent me back to 1969. I hadn't thought of them in years, Sally, Dick, and Jane—now it sounds like a porn film.

The meeting is over. I won't be back, but she'll give me a good recommendation. (It's Massachusetts law; believe me, she wouldn't if it weren't.) At least I don't have to be escorted out of the building by security guards; it's a WASPy, venerable old schoolhouse, after all; my crime, I suppose, is considered white-collar. White button-down collar.

I head back to my classroom to start packing my things up. I decide to leave the crepe and construction paper, and the mucilage and Elmer's glue. I'll take all my books. Going through the shelves, I take everything that's mine and leave anything with PROPERTY OF GRISWOLD SCHOOL, UPPER REACH, MA stamped across it.

Until I come across one lone copy of *Fun with Sally, Dick, and Jane*. What do you know? The old bat must have planted it here for me. I hold it in my hands, tracing my finger over the old, tattered cover—it's vintage 1962! Jane in barrettes and a pinafore, Sally in a poufy pink little dress, Dick in a red V-neck sweater and brown Oxfords. God, they're so . . . *white*. I guess I know where old Clara's politics stand . . .

Funny, I suddenly recall how I had kind of a crush on Dick when I was a kid reading these books. I open it up and start to read it, my head flooding with memories, but then I realize I need to finish up and get the hell out of the Griswold Penitentiary, so I return it to the shelf.

Wait . . . no. She wanted me to teach it, maybe she meant for me to have it. Even though it has PROPERTY OF . . . stamped all over it, I slide *Fun with Sally, Dick, and Jane* into my leather book satchel. I'll read it later, just for laughs and a little nostalgia.

And after that, I can sell it on eBay.

M Y SISTER Cynthia extends a kindly invitation to come and stay with her for a few days in Cambridge. She was divorced six months ago, so I'm sure she's invited me because she needs a man around the house to do some man things, even though she should know that I'm better at doing *men* than doing *man things*. Though not lately. "First grade teacher" simply does not sound like a sexy profession when it's spoken out loud in a gay bar. After seeing the look on the face of a potential trick/date/boyfriend, I usually add that a few years ago I spent a few months in the booby hatch when certain someones concluded that I was talking to myself more than usual. Alas, this hasn't worked too well, either. I guess Schizophrenic Elementary Education Specialist is not what the hunky men of Greater Gay Boston are looking for. At least, staying with Cynthia means I can spend time with my nephew Carlyle, who is six, the same age as my students at Griswold.

It's after dinner, and Carlyle has gone to bed; Cynthia and I are in the kitchen.

"So, Jason," she says, while scrubbing a pan with what I can only assume is premenopausal aggression, "do you want to talk about it?"

I figured this was coming. She's the big sister, after all, and our parents are gone.

"What would *it* be, my dear?" I say, thumbing through the *Globe* and pretending to be interested in local politics.

She turns to look at me.

"Oh, I don't know. Should we play Twenty Questions?"

"Well—"

"Just tell me one thing . . . did you lose your job because you had

. . . a spell, or something? I'm sorry, I don't know what else to call it."

"Jesus, Cynthia. You make me sound like something out of Tennessee Williams."

"Jason . . ."

"I was acting out *Alice in Wonderland.* I was playing all the parts— the White Queen, the Knave of Hearts. . . . I was switching voices. The children loved it. *God.*"

"Hmm . . ." she says, then runs her hand through her schoolgirl-ish, waist-length brown hair, which I think is too long for a woman her age, which is forty-two. "Maybe . . . maybe you went on a little too long . . . and you stopped . . . um . . . playing parts. Is that it?"

"Were you there, Cynthia?" I say. "I lost my job because of *cut-backs.* We're in economic doldrums right now. It says so right here in the *Globe.* Besides, it's a private school. There were too many first-grade teachers and not enough first-grade students. What were the teachers supposed to do, start teaching each other? I was not talking to myself." I know I shouldn't lie to her, but she'd run with the truth, or: she'd run after me with the truth, chasing me down with it and clobbering me over the head with it, and I'd rather keep her standing right where she is, so I can just walk away from her when I want to. Which, if she continues in this vein, is going to be soon.

"Well, that's funny then," she continues, "because you know your own history, Jason. And they say that kind of an . . . *affliction* usually repeats itself. Plus you've always had that weird fascination with books." She turns back to the sink and starts Brillo-padding the roasting pan even harder. I notice Cynthia uses Lemon Joy, which seems only half appropriate, since she *is* as sour as a lemon but possesses absolutely no joy whatsoever.

"Hello?" I practically shriek at her. "I *read.* I'm a *reader.* And I tried to teach the children to read, too. And, you know, since your reading life consists of a few store circulars and the *TV Guide,* I guess it's only natural you think that because I read substantial material, I'm weird."

She wheels around, wielding her dripping Brillo pad like a weapon. "You are in such denial, I can't believe it. And please don't shout. Do you want Carlyle to hear you?"

"That child could stand to read a book or two himself, instead of watching *Pokemon* 24/7."

For half a second, I think she's going to throw the Brillo pad at me. That would be something she'd do—throw a wet Brillo pad at someone and think it would have some kind of injurious effect. But she simply glares at me, then turns back around and resumes scrubbing, and scrubbing *furiously*.

"Don't tell me how to raise my child; I think I'm doing okay," she mutters with her back to me. "You have no idea what it's like to be a single mom."

This makes me feel a little sorry for her, all of a sudden, until she takes it upon herself to add this:

"And where Carlyle is concerned . . . I don't want him to see you talking to yourself like a . . . crazy person. He'll start to think he was born into a lunatic family. If you feel a spell coming on, or, a fit, you know, an *Alice in Wonderland* fit or whatever you're calling it, just make sure you don't have it in front of him."

That would be my cue to exit. I stomp upstairs to my room, which is Cynthia's attic, converted. It's too late to leave tonight and catch the bus back to my tiny little studio in Upper Reach, where I still have two months left on my lease, otherwise I'd be out the door. Passing Carlyle's room, I head up the stairs, open the door, and shut it, and try to lock it, but the lock is busted, which instantly reminds me of the time my parents took the lock off the door to my bedroom when I was thirteen because they thought I was smoking pot and whacking off to porno magazines. Which, of course, I was.

I lean against the door with my back to it, and suddenly I feel myself burning, about to fight back tears. Why does no one understand me? Why can't anyone see past my occasional—okay, dammit, *spells*—and think that maybe instead of crazy, I'm just creative? And eccentric, sort of like . . . I don't know . . . the love child of Auntie Mame and Captain Kangaroo. Oh, those repressed, tweedy, dunderheaded schoolmarms at Griswold! I can just see them all, trudging back there in September, job security and antiquated teaching methods intact, while I serve up the Millionaire's Breakfast—"I'm Jason, and I'll be your server this morning"—to a bunch of weary travelers at the IHOP on the interstate. Is that what's to become of me? Oh, I can't help but feel that those old marms all waged a campaign to get rid of me and persuaded their like-minded coven head Miss Clara that I was unfit for the classroom. I feel just like Rosemary and her baby—everyone is against me, and Miss Griswold is Ruth Gordon! And I don't even have a hunky husband like John Cassevettes. Worst-case scenario! If I'm going to be drafted by a bunch of witches and impregnated with the Devil's baby, I should at least get a night of sex out of it.

How can they think I'm crazy, that I'm having spells? I gave those six-year-olds their first taste of performance art, and some old fogey focuses instead on my one five-minute collapse when I thought Richard Gere was breaking up with me. *He's talking to himself, Miss Griswold. I'd call that a nervous breakdown. Shouldn't he be asked to leave?* Oh, I should just take my act to New York and the East Village; they appreciate performance art down there.

I throw myself onto the bed, an old metal-framed single, the perfect size for a boy, a joint, and a magazine, just like it was in our old house. Then I realize this *is* my old bed—Cynthia must have taken it after Dad died. How appropriate, and boy, do I wish I had that joint. *A weird relationship with books!* How dare she say that to me. The nerve of her. Of all of them. Books are your only real friends anyway.

I wonder, actually, if I do have a joint in my satchel. I open it up and rummage around. No luck, only . . .

Fun with Sally, Dick, and Jane. Jeez.

Do I really need to read this? I mean, I'm not going to be teaching it, or anything else, at the Griswold School, so . . . oh, why not? I do remember thinking Dick was a hottie once upon a time . . .

I open it up, for the first time in twenty-five years . . .

There they are, the sisters, sitting at a little table, the little green table in the red, yellow, and blue kitchen, having teatime with plastic, doll-like cups and saucers. They are just as I remember them. They don't notice me at all; they're much too busy talking. I have no problem with eavesdropping on them; it's my book now, after all.

"Dick has gotten so much worse, you know, Sal?" Jane is saying to

Sally. She leans back and puffs on a cigarette, blowing smoke rings. "I mean, just when I thought he was finally going to start communicating like an adult, he reverts back to three-word sentences. Jesus."

"I know," Sally replies, sighing and tossing her sunbeam-yellow Shirley Temple ringlets coquettishly. "But that *is* how he was raised to speak, after all."

"Hey, we were raised that way too!" Jane shoots back. "But you and I transcended it. Well, at least *I* have."

"I have too, Jane!" Sally counters, with a trace of little-girl poutiness. "The only time I play with dolls now is when a child picks up the book and reads us!"

"Yeah, whatever," Jane says, stubbing out her cigarette on the bottom of her left patent leather Mary Jane. She goes immediately for another one, from a packet concealed in her pinafore. "All I know is, I'm a forty-seven-year-old woman trapped in the body of an eleven-year-old girl. This is my sexual prime, for God's sake!"

"From what I understand, most women would feel lucky to have that kind of a problem," Sally says, projecting bright optimism. "Look at it this way: you'll never have to go under the knife to look younger. I mean, look at Mom. She's seventy-nine and looks perpetually thirty-two."

"Easy for you to say, Sal. You're nine; you never reached puberty. It's different for you."

"Oh, Jane, you're so negative. And I don't know why. I mean, you're lucky you got to go through puberty! You got to develop. And you have Dick, and Dick is cute, and you always say he never turns you down when you're—what is it called?—'in the mood.'"

"He's my *brother*, for God's sake! Is this my lot in life? Sex with my brother for the rest of my natural existence? Christ!"

"But you say he's good."

Jane thinks a moment. "Well, he isn't bad, that's true . . . even though lately, he seems less interested. But what do I have to compare it to?"

"Well," Sally muses. "You did tell me about that one night when Dad got a little—"

"Hold it right there, little sister," Jane says, pointing the cigarette in Sally's direction. "I told you we were never mentioning that again."

"Sorry," Sally says, meekly.

After a moment, Jane says. "Okay, okay, it's not the sex. The sex is fine. Sort of. It's the afterglow."

"The what?" Sally asks, confused but still perky.

"You know, after it's over, you want a man to say all the right . . . um . . . *sentences*," Jane says, idly brushing an ash off her otherwise pristine white pinafore. "And the thing is, Dick was really coming along. He was starting to compliment me afterwards, saying things like, 'Gosh, Jane, that felt amazing', you know, use larger words. But now he's regressed, it's back to 'Suck Jane. See Jane suck Dick.' Stuff like that. Makes me nuts." This causes her to start puffing even more furiously on her cigarette, with a faraway look in her eyes; she seems to be considering something deeply.

"Sometimes you seem wise beyond your years, Jane."

Jane throws Sally a withering look. "That's exactly my point! Oh, God. Am I the only person around here who understands *irony*?" she moans.

At this moment, Spot, the family dog, strolls in. He is black and white, and friendly.

"See Spot!" exclaims Sally, clearly regressing in the wake of Jane's existential anger. A safety valve?

"Sally, we're not being read now. You can relate to Spot on an adult level."

"Bow Wow!" barks Spot.

"See Spot bark," Sally says, chuckling and tossing curls.

"Jesus Christ," says Jane.

Now this is where I break in. "Excuse me," I say.

Both girls look up, startled, then they slowly turn out front, off the page. They peer out at me like actors from a stage—wide-eyed and frightened, as if caught by an intruder. Which, of course, I am.

"Who are you?" Jane asks, quickly putting out her cigarette and waving telltale smoke away. "You're not a school-aged child!"

"Growlllllllllll . . ." growls Spot but it's not very menacing. Cujo he's not.

"Calm down, you stupid mongrel," Jane hisses.

"I couldn't help overhearing. I think I can help."

"Oh yeah?" Jane says. "How?"

"Well, I think I understand your . . . situation. I have sibling troubles myself."

"See Spot. Spot barks. Hear Spot bark," Sally says, visibly nervous.

"Quiet, Sally, it's okay," Jane says, ever the big sister. And then back to me: "I'd like to hear your suggestions, actually."

"Well . . . what I thought was——"

And at this moment, I hear my six-year-old nephew Carlyle come bounding up the attic stairs; he's in my room in lightning speed.

"Whatcha doin', Uncle Jason?" he asks, dropping his ball on the floor and letting it roll over to me.

Immediately, and no doubt out of a learned sense of duty to young readers, Jane, Sally, and Spot snap to attention, suddenly freezing on the page in a "playtime" tableau.

"Carlyle, I had no idea you were still up."

"I'm still up. But Mom doesn't know, so . . ." He makes the shush sound, his fingers to his lips. "Whatcha doin'?" he whispers.

"Just reading an old book. Would you like to read it with me? I think you might like it."

He eyes me suspiciously. "Okay."

He bounds over to me, and we sit down on the floor with our backs against the bottom of the iron bed frame.

"This is called *Fun with Sally, Dick, and Jane*, and when I was your age, this was my favorite book."

"Are the Rugrats in it?" Carlyle asks. I glance quickly at the page, and I'm sure I can almost see Jane suppressing a cynical smirk

"Nah, but it's good anyway," I tell him. And I start to read. " 'See Sally. See Jane. See Jane and Sally play. Play Jane. Play Sally. Fun, fun, fun!'"

"Whose dog?" Carlyle asks.

"I'm getting to that. 'Here is Spot. See Spot. Run Spot! Spot barks. Bow Wow. Hear Spot bark.'"

But Carlyle is restless, squirming. "This is boring," he says, rolling his eyes.

"I like the Rugrats. I'll get *Rugrats Go to Paris*." And he gets up and runs out of the room and back down the stairs. Then I hear Cynthia intercepting him downstairs; he won't be back tonight.

"He didn't like us," says Sally, when Carlyle is out of earshot.

"Oh please, what else is new?" Jane snaps. "We haven't been a major cultural force, let alone a teaching tool, for twenty years. We're relics, Sally. Museum pieces. Has-beens! But I don't really give a damn, you know? I mean, do I really want to compete with something called a "Rugrat"? A *Rugrat*?!! I don't think so."

"Don't be so dramatic, Jane," I say. "You're a permanent part of American popular culture, and you should know there's been quite a resurgence of interest lately in your series, and—"

"Whatever," she says, cutting me off. "As far as I'm concerned, as soon as *Sesame Street* hit the airwaves, we were toast."

"Well, I'm not sure it's—"

"Say, you look fairly intelligent," she says, interrupting again. "You probably get what's going on here. So what can you do for me? Because if Dick doesn't stop talking baby-talk, I'm gonna lose my mind, you know? It's bad enough being trapped in an incestuous relationship; does it have to be a monosyllabic one too?"

"It's not so different with men in the real world, quite frankly," I say. "At least, that's been my experience."

"Oh really?" Jane says, looking at me with a knowing smirk.

"What does he mean?" Sally asks.

"Never mind, you're too young," says Big Sister.

"I'm forty-two!" says Sally.

"You're *nine*!" Jane barks. See Jane bark. *Bark, Jane, bark.*

"Would you like a change of scene, Jane?" I ask.

At this, Jane really takes me in, narrowing her gaze and looking suspicious. "You're kidding me, right? You mean you can actually get me out of—" (and here she casts a dismissive glance at Sally) "— Candyland?"

"I could."

"Jane, you can't leave . . ." Sally says and begins to cry.

"Put a lid on it, kid, I'm tired of your codependency," Jane says. "Bigger and better opportunities are about to come my way. I always knew I was destined for bigger and better things. Who knew this was my lucky day? So . . ." She turns her attention back to me. "What do we do?"

"Well, first," I say, "I need some time alone with Dick."

Another smirk slowly crosses her face, and she folds her arms. "Oh yeah? Is that so?"

I must say, for a drawing, she's pretty intuitive. "Well, be my guest. But Dick is a real guy. He likes to do real guy kinds of things. You know, play catch, cut the grass, stuff like that. You don't look like you're really the type to——"

"I do just fine in that department, thank you," I tell her. "Be nice, or you're staying right here in the family hour."

"Fine. But can I make a request, please? In my new digs—no *primary colors*! I'm sick of them. Sick to death of them. Please . . . earth tones! Some nice beiges and neutrals."

"I'll work on it. Now I'm gonna go talk to Dick."

"Page 19. He's mowing the lawn, and I think his shirt is unbuttoned."

HE'S THERE, of course, right where she said he'd be. Right as I had remembered him, an all-American boy, about fourteen, pushing the old kind of nonmotorized lawn cutter (not the scary, clunky, gasoline-filled ones I had to use) over Astroturf-colored green grass, with his red cowboy shirt halfway unbuttoned down his smooth, pinkish chest. He is smiling and sunny, on a smiling and sunny perfect summer day, the skies as blue as his jeans; the big, puffy clouds the same white of his pearl-sparkly teenage teeth. The very picture of nonsweating, cheerful, chore-doing boy happiness. He's the kind of guy I always wanted to be, desperately, but never was. He's also the kind of boy I always wanted to . . . *have* but was never able to get.

"Good day for cutting the grass," I say.

He stops mowing, looks out blankly, considers me for a moment, and says:

"Dick mows the grass. See Dick mow! Mow, Dick, mow. Mow, mow, mow!"

"Oh, please, Dick," I say. "Really now."

But he smiles and just waves. Is there perhaps the slightest trace of uncertainty in his eyes?

"You were my first love, you know," I continue. "When I was six and went to school, this was my first book. And there you were, so much older than me, so athletic, such an Eagle Scout, such a doer of good deeds . . . I thought about you all the time."

Now Dick looks disgusted. Should this surprise me? He goes back to cutting the grass, but, I note, a little less cheerfully than before.

"I'm sorry. I shouldn't have said all that, I guess," I say, backpedaling. After all, I don't want him to dislike me. And surely Dick, of all people, can't dismiss me simply because I'm a first grade teacher. "I really just wanted to be friends."

He keeps mowing. Clackkclackkkclackkclackkkkclackkk. . . . .

"I've been talking to Jane. She's very unhappy. She'd like to make a change, and I've promised to help her."

At this, he stops. And after a moment, says:

"Dick is helpful. Dick likes to help. See Dick help. See Dick help Jane. See Dick help Sally. Help, Dick, help."

"I'm losing patience with this," I snap. "You're practically in your fifties, for God's sake. Which means that I'm not doing anything illegal lusting after your fourteen-year-old body, because, in reality, what this really is, if you look at it, say, in role-playing terms, is a dad-son kind of thing. Except, even though I'm thirty-three, you're the dad and I'm the son. Sorry, it's complicated."

He looks blankly at me again but does not resume mowing. And why should he? The grass never grows, after all. I seem to actually have his attention.

"Jane tells me you had graduated to compound sentences, which made her happy, but now you've regressed back to subject-verb, and, on a good day, subject-verb-object. My guess here is that you're tired of Jane, and, quite frankly, she *is* a little fishwifey, even though she's your sister and only thirteen."

At this he actually frowns and looks away, off into the distance.

"Okay, whatever. My theory is that neither of you has had enough experimentation. With other people, I mean. I also think you're trying to distance yourself from her, and that this faux-regression thing is your way of getting out of whatever it is between the two of you that doesn't make you feel satisfied. I also think you understand every word I'm saying. Is that right, Dick?"

He looks at me a moment. And then, ever cheerful, he says: "Dick says good-bye. Wave, Dick, wave. Wave good-bye! Wave, wave, wave!"

"All right, Dick," I say, because I'm always such a pushover where good-looking, slightly addled young-old men are concerned, "but I'll be back."

And I think there's a look of recognition in his eyes as I turn the page.

WHEN I LOCATE Jane and Sally again, it is Sally who wants to talk.

"I'm very concerned about that little boy," she says.

"Carlyle? Why?"

"We had no effect on him at all," she says, clearly having given this some thought.

"Oh, Sal," Jane says. "It's not like we haven't accomplished any-thing over the years, for God's sake. Think of all the illiterate six-year-olds we taught to read. We've done our jobs; what's wrong with retirement? Besides, it's time for new adventures and greener pas-tures, and honey, I, for one, am ready for that."

"I'm not ready to retire, Jane," Sally says softly, shaking her yellow head and looking down.

Jane has changed into a pink and white polka dot jumper (A-lined, with kick pleats) over a short-sleeved white Peter Pan–collar blouse, white patent leather Mary Janes, white ankle socks with pink piping, a big, flouncy pink bow on one side of her hair, a large white barrette on the other.

"I'm ready to go, kid," Jane says to me, after twirling and model-ing, clearly having put some major consideration into this outfit. "What do you think?"

"It's not exactly Valentino, but it will do, I suppose."

"And just what do you mean by that?"

"Well . . . don't you think bow *and* barrette is overkill?"

She narrows her eyes, and her lips curl into a smirking snarl. "Excuse me. You think I don't know what I'm doing? I set the standard for American little girl fashion for over twenty years. Twenty years!"

"Well . . ."

"So I'm quite certain I'm ready to go . . . off, off, off!"

"Will she be okay?" Sally asks. "Will she come back?"

"Yes," I assure her. I have a sister of my own, for what it's worth. "Think of it as a mini-vacation."

"So what do we do?" Jane asks, touching up her hair and smoothing her skirt.

"I have a plan," I say.

And I take a pair of scissors and begin to cut out the half of the page where Jane stands.

"Ooh, be careful with that thing!" Sally squeals. She runs to the corner of the page, trembling.

"Not to worry," I say, as I successfully separate Jane from her surroundings.

"Free at last!" she exclaims, in my palm a pink Fay Wray talking to a WASP King Kong.

"Bye Jane," Sally says, mournful. "Sally waves bye. 'Bye Jane. Wave, wave, wave."

"Oh for God's sake, Sally. Compound sentences! Dependent clauses! Dangling participles! You can handle it."

"Wave, Sally, wave," Sally says, barely audible.

"Oh well. See ya, kid," Jane says, waving back.

Now I open up an old, tattered copy of *The Adventures of Huckleberry Finn* to a two-page spread illustration of Huck and Jim on the raft, rowing down the Mississippi. Slowly, I float Jane down onto the raft.

"Oh my," she says, touching down, getting her bearings.

"Have fun, Jane. Back to you in a little while."

"Oh my," Jane says, already eager, already *belonging*, as Huck and Jim both turn, wide-eyed, to look at her . . .

I'M AT THE breakfast table the next morning; Carlyle is outside playing, and Cynthia and I are sitting in silence.

"Okay, I apologize," I say, finally. "Whatever I did, I apologize."

"Me too," she says, meekly. We can both see Carlyle from the kitchen window, playing in his sandbox. He waves. Wave, Carlyle, wave.

"Just tell me one thing," she says. "Because I thought I heard . . . were you talking to yourself last night? It's all right if you were, really . . ."

"Oh, that. Well, yes. I was rehearsing a monologue," I say. "I'm going to be in a play with the Upper Reach Community Theatre League. *Our Town.*"

She eyes me, warily, then brightens. "Well, that's nice. That'll take your mind off losing your job."

THERE IS A PAGE in the Sally, Dick, and Jane book that got my six-year-old heart thumping years ago. In the drawing, Dick has finished mowing the lawn and is relaxing in the hammock, drinking a lemonade that Mother (perfectly coifed, in high heels, frilly dress, and apron) has brought to him on a serving tray on the previous page. Dick's shirt is unbuttoned all the way, and he has taken off his shoes and socks; he swings the hammock gently with his pink-white all-American feet. Naturally, he has not broken a sweat.

When I get to the page, he is there, just as I have remembered him.

"Hello, Dick," I say, and I'm sure the telltale touch of hoarseness in my throat announces my intentions.

He focuses his blue eyes in my direction, studying me. He wiggles his toes and sips his lemonade. Is this a tease?

"What have you done with my sister?" he says, finally.

"So you *can* communicate," I say, exhaling a sigh of relief. After all, it doesn't usually take me *this* long to get a good-looking man to talk to me.

"Of course I can," he says. "But why should I talk to you? You're an unwanted interloper. I didn't trust you the first time you came to talk to me and I don't trust you now. You have no business here with us, now that you're a grown-up. But I'm concerned for my sister, so I have to talk to you."

"Oh? Well, *Jane* seems grateful for my . . . intrusions. I'm sorry you're not. You're my favorite, after all."

He rolls his eyes at me.

"I'll let that pass," he says. "This is very serious. Sally and I have discussed this, and we can't let Mother and Father know. They're very fragile people, beneath that controlled exterior. Knowing that Jane is gone would totally rock their world."

"I gave Jane what she wanted. An adventure."

"Jane is a mixed-up middle-aged woman who doesn't know what she wants. She wants to have sex with her own brother, for God's sake."

"Well, obviously you're more than willing to comply," I retort, angry that this isn't going according to my plan.

He thinks a minute. Then: "You think this is lemonade, don't you?" he says, pointing to the icy, sweating glass in his hand.

"Yes."

"Wrong. Vodka. On the rocks. We color it yellow, to fool the children. Mother makes a good, stiff cocktail. We're all drinkers here."

"Oh?"

"Think about it. Wouldn't you be if you lived here?"

"Well—"

"Jane talks a good game about our sexual relationship," he continues. "Actually, she lies. Quite frankly, it's never really gone beyond adolescent brother-sister experimentation, but she likes to pretend it has, and seems to enjoy embellishing the story to anyone who will listen. I'm sure she said something about Dad, too, about . . . *that*. Not true at all. Dad is impotent. He goes to a job, but we have no idea what that job is. Then he comes home and sits in a chair and reads a newspaper with no news in it. He hardly even speaks to Mom. It wouldn't even occur to him to have a sexual thought about anyone. He's . . . well, he's very remote."

His voice trails off here, and he looks down into his glass, silent for a moment.

"I . . . I think I understand," I tell him. "No . . . I definitely understand."

He looks back up at me and after a moment says, "So you see Jane fabricates stories to make her life sound more interesting. It's all right, she's entitled to have an imagination. Actually, she's more imaginative than the people who drew us originally, which is where her resentment comes from. And you may have noticed how much she hates monosyllabism?"

"Yes, she mentioned it," I say, all ears.

"Well, that's not something that bothers me. It's our native language, I have no problem with it. But it gets her rattled, for some reason. Jane is a self-loathing educational tool. So whenever she gets too intense around me, to turn her off, I talk in simple sentences. She thinks I'm regressing, but it's all very calculated, on my part. I don't think that . . . well, I don't think it's right for brothers and sisters to . . . we were drawn in a moral universe, after all."

"I see . . . you mean, Jane has never actually been . . . has never completely had . . . Oh my God."

"Is there a problem?" Dick asks, draining his drink.

"Well, I don't know . . . but I probably need to go see about her."

He stares at me. Hard. "Who are you?" he asks. "What do you want with us?"

This takes me by surprise. I stammer: "I don't know . . . I'm just a guy. A first-grade teacher. Unemployed. Who likes to read." I feel my face go hot; as red, I'm sure, as Sally's little wagon parked in the corner of the page.

Dick snorts. "'Likes to read.' That's a euphemism for lonely, if you ask me. How sad. You turn to a first-grade primer for sexual gratification! Son, you need to get a life. Or at least go on the Internet."

"Now wait a second, Dick, I—"

"You like me, don't you?" he says. "I fuel some twisted childhood fantasy for you, don't I?"

"Look, Dick," I stammer again. "I was a sexually aware child, early on. I masturbated very early. Earlier than most. And you were kind of the first, you know, visual aid that I had. I'm sorry, I . . ."

"I'm old enough to be your father," he says, looking genuinely disgusted.

"I know . . . well, maybe that's part of it, too, I don't know . . . it's—"

"Do you like my feet?"

"What?"

"My feet. You like them, don't you? And my chest, too?"

"I guess I do."

"You're out of control. What did you expect, barging in here? Did you think we could have *sex*, you and I? Did you even think it was in the realm of possibility? And did you think that I, the ultimate red-blooded, all-American boy, would actually want to have sex with you?"

"I always thought red-blooded all-American boys were the best kind," I say, suddenly ashamed, but why?

He grins and brushes a lock of brown hair off his forehead, which makes me shiver. Every straight man is a flirt if he knows you're interested. Even cartoons.

"Well, if you wanna sit there and whack off and look at me, there's not much I can do about it," he tells me. "Except to remind you of how pathetic that is."

I hang my head. It's like being lectured . . . by your dad.

"We did our part for you," he continues. "We taught you to read. That's our function. What we do in our world behind closed book covers is our business."

"I guess you're right . . ."

"And if the world you live in hadn't changed so drastically, so regrettably, we could still teach that snotty little boy who was here earlier to read. But our time has passed. Let us rest now."

"God, Dick, you're practically elegiac," I say. "I'm impressed."

"You always were. You were part of the last generation we had any effect on. Too bad you turned out the way you did. But I suppose you could learn to do better. Now about my sister . . ."

"I'll take care of it. I promise."

He smiles and leans back in the hammock, flexing his feet and dropping his hand to his smooth chest, peering at me with clear, thick-lashed blue eyes.

"Good boy," he says.

I AM TERRIFIED of what I may find when I go to open up *Huckleberry Finn*. With shaking fingers, I flip ahead to the dog-eared page, Jim and Huck sailing on the river into the sunset.

It's worse than I imagined. The three of them, sprawled on the raft, spent, exhausted, disheveled, but glowing, and smoking cigarettes.

"Jane?" I whisper.

She looks up at me, all sleepy, hooded eyes, bangs falling over her forehead in Veronica Lake mode. The barrette is lopsided. The pink hair ribbon, I notice, is now tied around Huckleberry's neck, underneath his ear-to-ear grin.

"Yes?" she says, in a whiskey voice. "Do I know you?"

"Don't be ridiculous," I say. "It's time to go home. I've made a mistake. I should never have let this happen."

She sits up and glares at me.

"I can't leave now. We're going to travel down the river, just me and the boys."

Huck and Jim nuzzle up to either side of Jane, quite the threesome.

Huck, of course, doesn't stay closed-mouthed about anything, so he instantly pipes up. "This here Jane's 'bout the purtiest gal young'un I ever saw," he opines. "Beats all heck outa that stuck-up ol' Becky Thatcher any ol' day, I'll tell you what's the truth. And Miss Jane here puts out more, too." And he slobbers a big, sloppy adolescent wet kiss on Jane, who feigns distaste but allows it anyway.

"Hold on now, Huckleberry," Jim says, in his Old Man River baritone. "Don' be sayin' nuffin' get us in no trouble now, y'heah?"

And he too cozies up to Miss Jane, on the other side. So much for those postmodern revisionist theories about the *real* nature of Huck and Jim's relationship. This is pure, unadulterated heterosexuality, and I, for one, feel unwelcome.

"Heaven, sheer heaven," Jane says, cupping both their faces with her hands and throwing her head back, tossing bangs and laughing vampishly.

"Tell the boys good-bye, Jane," I say, as I begin to carefully excise her from this picturesque little tableau. "It's time to go home."

And she is in my palm again, and I return Huck and Jim back to their real business on the Mississippi River, despite their loud, animalistic protests, which ebb and die out as I close the cover over them.

"I'm not going home!" Jane shrieks from my palm. "After that, do you really think I could go back to Prettyville? Land of the gleaming and the sanitized? I'm a woman of the world, now. I'm experienced!"

"Jane . . ."

"Oh please," she begs. "One more, please? I've got a whole list now. Huck and Jim were telling me about all these single guys. For instance, I'm just dying to meet Robinson Crusoe! Sounds like just my kind of man. Burly, brawny . . ."

"Jane, you're a pint-sized nymphet," I say. "But I do think I can give you one more outing."

"Yes, yes," Jane says, fluffing her hair and readjusting her barrette and jumper. "I knew you'd listen to reason."

"This will be a little different, but I think it'll be good for you."

"Tell me, tell me."

And I carry Jane to the bookshelf where I look alphabetically through the As, though Carlyle has done some rearranging, and they're out of order. Aristotle, Auden, Austen, . . .

I finally find the one I'm looking for. "Here it is," I tell her. "Alcott, Louisa May."

A FEW HOURS LATER, I open up *Little Women*. I have placed Jane in a beautiful illustration of the March girls sitting by the fireside on a cold, snowy New England winter's night. All hearty and hearthy. The girls are mostly sewing (Jo is reading) or playing primitive nineteenth-century games.

"Jesus Christ, I thought you'd never come back!" Jane bellows when she sees me, breaking the lovely, somber mood.

The March girls look up from their tasks, startled.

"Hush up, girl," says Amy to Jane, "and stoke the fire. For warmth."

"That's another thing. It's cold as a witch's tit in here!" Jane reports, loudly.

"My, my, how disagreeable!" says Meg. "And after Beth and Amy have spent the entire evening knitting you a warm woolen sweater, too." She *tsk-tsks*.

"This is *soooo boring*," Jane continues. "Are you aware," she says to me, "that there are no men here?"

"Jane, do you really know Huckleberry Finn?" asks Jo suddenly, looking up from her book. "What's he like?"

"Oh, sister, you have no idea," Jane begins.

"All right, all right," I say. "I'll take you back. I just thought after what happened to you on the Mississippi River, you could use a little snow, not to mention female companionship, to cool you off."

"You thought wrong. Get me out of here."

"Leaving so soon, Janey?" Beth asks, frail but loving. "Why you've hardly even touched your cider!" Jane throws her a withering look.

"Jane, why don't you thank the Marches for their hospitality?" I say. "Your mother would want you to do that."

Jane shoots me a look of daggers. But then, because she was drawn well, after all, says: "Thank you all for your hospitality."

"Good health and Godspeed, Jane," says Amy, still knitting, "and come calling again, won't you?"

"Yeah, right," Jane mutters, as I extract her from the March fireside and carry her carefully back to Sally and Dick.

"YOU'RE BACK!" Sally exclaims, as I reposition Jane in her rightful place on the page. In this scene, Dick and Sally are romping with Spot and Puff, the kitten, on the freshly mown green Astroturf grass.

"Romp, Jane, romp," I say.

"See Jane play," says Dick.

"Okay, look Dick," says Jane. "I guess it's no secret that I've had other men now, on this little holiday I've taken. And quite frankly, you kind of pale in comparison, if you know what I mean."

"I don't know about that, " I say, dreamily. He shoots me a sharp look, but then it softens into a slight smile at the corners of his perfect mouth. Maybe we're friends after all.

"Well, whatever," Jane says, pushing Puff disdainfully in Sally's direction. "So, you know, I kind of think it's over between us, in that way. I mean, after Huck and Jim . . ." But then, she glazes over for a moment, lost in remembering. Sally and Dick respectfully look away, allowing Jane her reverie. Then she continues: "But then, who can figure out what the hell Huck Finn is saying anyway, I mean what kind of illiterate gobbledygook is that? I kept telling him he needs to read us, but he claims he never wants to learn to read. Can you believe that? Oh well, I guess that means he's probably not the right man for me after all. But I'll say one thing for Huck, he isn't mono-syllabic!"

"Hmm . . ." I say. "What about the grunts?"

"You keep out of this," she says. She turns back to her brother.

"So listen, Dick," she continues. "Enough of the monosyllabal-ism, all right? I mean, unless in the *remote* chance some child ever wants to read us again . . ."

"I'm glad to have my sister back," says Dick, and he gives her a big brother hug and looks pleased.

"About that child part," says Sally. "I think we should try again, with that little boy."

The three of them turn to me, awaiting my reaction.

"Do you think we could teach him something? Maybe?" asks Sally.

"Oh, why not?" Jane says. "But, hey, kid!" she says to me. "Give us a build-up, you know? Some decent PR. We need it."

"Okay," I say." "Can you get ready for him?" And in no time, the three of them are in their places, looking clean, fresh, young, ready to go. Jane throws me a quick wink, then turns her complete attention back to the wagon. Sally plays with Puff, and Dick . . . Dick is drinking "lemonade" in the hammock. Ah. . . . appearances are everything. And Dick is right; whose business is it what goes on behind closed book covers?

As I go to get Carlyle, I suddenly hear his voice outside my door. He's talking to my sister.

"But Uncle Jason said he would read to me, Mom!"

"Carlyle, I want you to leave your Uncle Jason alone for a while," I hear Cynthia say. "Go downstairs and watch TV."

"But I'd rather read!"

"Carlyle, I've told you. Your uncle isn't feeling well . . . and . . . well, it'll be better if you just go downstairs. I'll go down with you." And I hear the two of them descend the stairs to the family room, their voices distancing.

I walk back over to the bed and pick up the open book.

"What's going on?" Jane asks, speaking under her breath, still poised over the wagon and looking "sweet."

"Well . . . I guess he's not going to read you right now."

The three of them drop their stances. Puff makes a beeline for the sandbox and starts scratching.

"If not now, when?" asks Dick.

"I don't know."

"That's too bad," he says. "This would have been a good time. We're perfect again."

Listen, Jason, listen. See, Jason, see.

"I'll just have to get back to you on when," I say.

"Well . . ." Jane says, "you know where we'll be." And she exhales a world-weary sigh and sits in the wagon, cupping her chin in her hands and looking down at the ground.

"Yes, I hope we can help," says Sally. She gets up from the grass and wanders over to the hammock. Dick offers her lemonade. She accepts, and then drains it.

"I'll get Mom to make some more," he says quietly and heads in the direction of the house.

"Last call, huh, Dick?" I say.

He pauses at the door. "No such thing as last call here, sport," he says, and goes inside.

Jane continues to stare at the ground, and Sally gazes far off into the blue sky and puffy white clouds. It seems like a good time to close the cover, so I do.

"See Jason learn," I say to myself, as I lie down on my bed. Ah . . . talking to myself after all. Well, what do you know.

See Jason learn.

Learn, Jason!

Learn, learn, learn!

Reasons to Stop

You reach into a dirty toilet to retrieve your lipstick

You get into a fist fight with a metal gate outside of a Ukrainian diner
at four am

You pick up a man in a lesbian bar

Your cat silently speaks to you in Spanish

The word "happenstance" is written across your hand in the
morning

You stand in the middle of Twenty-third Street on a Saturday night
screaming "Why won't you have sex with me?"

Your beer goggles wear whiskey goggles

Happy Hours make you want to punch holes through plate
glass windows

You wake up in some girl's apartment, one wrist tied to a white
wicker couch beneath a poster of Kenny G

You call your mother to see if she can tell how high you are

You call your dealer "mom" by mistake

You call the bartender "faggot" when he won't serve you anymore

Your friend, you know, that one with the serious substance abuse
problem, puts you in a cab

You can't remember what Sunday looks like

Then there are the nights you walk through the streets crying
And there are already enough women in this city with tears in
   their eyes

miscellaneous Rifts on Friction—
(meant to acknowledge some)

Would you love me if I mimicked you/
called you out of your name/
wore ya mama's hair on stage/
made you feel insane?

The first friction matches were composed of a compound of chlorate of potash and sugar mixed with powdered gum arabic to make it adhesive when applied to a splinter of wood. They were ignited by drawing them rapidly and under considerable pressure through a piece of sandpaper.

Do some white butches have an obsession with Black dildos? Is it okay? Is it fucked up? Is it disturbing? How many pictures of Asian, Latina, and Black dykes have you ever seen with white dildos on the pages of magazines?

What do we do in the presence of friction? Run? Hide? Pull our parts away from each other and say we tried? Do we rub harder in order to identify the source of heat and spark? Do we get burned? Have scars? Do we jump down into the middle of it? Do we say we've seen it, seen it all before and proceed to describe how it was the last time in intimate detail? Do we say we've never seen it before? Didn't know it existed?

Strom Thurmond died last night. I opened up a bottle of
champagne to toast with my ancestors.

What is a relatively racist act? A nearly racist act?

My house/my skin/my sister is burning again.
You lit the match. You were only playing. But I'm burning again anyway.

Are you gonna stand there explaining how this flame is different,
    less hot, less damaging because you didn't mean to do it?
While I'm burning, are you gonna ask me to explain why I'm cry-
    ing the same way my father cried, while I'm wailing the same
    way my mama did? Are you going to demand that I'm okay. Tell
    me that it ain't that bad getting burnt up because it ain't like it
    happened on purpose? Are you going to write your dissertation
    with my ashes?

You can always call the fire truck,
You know they'll come quicker if you call
You could douse what you did. And
Apologize.
Help me rebuild my house the way I want it built—
With or without your hands touching it.
We could examine the damage later/ separately/ together some-
    times, maybe//

but I don't want to be near your hollow excuses.
I want you to tell your people to stop playing with matches if they
    can't contain the damage in their own bodies.

Would you love me if I cared enough to tell you your shit was
    fucked up

CARL MORSE

On a Christmas Card that Came Back Stamped "Deceased"

In memoriam: Lester Tweedie

I think you probably killed yourself
as a final favor to the world
("Now would I ever do a think like that?")
plus your solemn vow not to eat any extra shit.

Last spring you staggered into town
holding your insides in and your outsides up
and the whole bar down.
Was it AIDS?
Some final affection for a fist?
Or just "the old ticker," free at last?

Their weapons were ridicule and rope.
Yours was being a lover that went for broke
then refused to cry over anything spilt
—like the eggs across your windshield,
like three grown sons not speaking to their queer dad,
like its getting advertised all over town
like the funny horns blaring past your house at night,
like the blood in your mouth at Burger King.

But you fought back with the biggest birthday cakes
the neighbors had ever seen,
with a condom on every candlestick,
and a verbal life like joyous rats
springing at unexpected cheese,
while copping slow feels that, rooted, charmed,
the studs were amazed they let you have,
not to mention the kids you sent back, armed,
to their scrimmage piles and ranchmobiles.

You called for help just once,
leaping at me from the truck,
going for all the vital parts,
making me hit you and hang on tight
until you stopped biting and drank my spit.

Then we both hung on to that child all night,
snow in the walls and hate on the stair,
and brothers that rassled like hungry bears,
and a mom you loved behind her back
and a dad you drilled to death in dreams
—drowning the kittens in the sink,
slicing off warts with the butcher knife,
throwing back suckers, keeping eels,
outspelling the bastards at every turn.

That fall, at an unmarked fairy den,
you swore at the oven hard enough
to make it feed us all,
while driving off straights who wandered in,
saying it was a leper colony
and that they were entirely welcome to stay,
refusing all compliments for a week,
sneaking into the group hug at the end.

Then you were the clearest, fiercest, best,
right after the Christians came with guns
to sanctify my house and me
—offering to sugar their tanks,
loosen their drive shafts,
skin their brats,
shove hilarious things up their sick holes.

Lester, we loved you
even when we couldn't guess
where you'd strike out next
or tell yet another dirty lie
about what you deserved.

You didn't fool a blessèd soul
with your fake castrations or your farts,
and no new kick in the gut can change that now.

Gay Nigger Number One

In memoriam Steen Keith Fenrich

> "Yonder they do not love your flesh. They despise it. They
> don't love your eyes, they'd just as soon pick em out. No
> more do they love the skin on your back. Yonder they flay
> it. And O my people they do not love your hands. Those
> they only use, tie, bind, chop off and leave empty. Love
> your hands! Love them. Raise them up and kiss them."
>
> —Baby Suggs, *Beloved*, Toni Morrison

In this season of blood
I try to harvest
life from your planted body

Spring cherry trees bloom
thousands of dove-white skulls
Branches rattle down loose teeth
The sun sorrow hot
as I carry your ghost
heavy in my arms

I am just a poet
my words brittle
against the mad butcher's knife
that cut away at your lips with
exact delicacy
skinning deep
violet plums

Your hands forever disappeared
Brown sweet pomegranate fingertips

stolen by that ghoul
your mother loved

All he left was
your skull bleached of color
scrawled with the words
Gay Nigger Number One

Too strange a fruit
for the cover of *Time*
the country collaborates
bleaches your name off the page

Steen last night
I heard your screams in
each drop of rain

If I were Isis
I would gather up your
hacked-to-bits body
weep you alive

"

What possible future could we have? Two intelligent, beautiful women (my grandmother taught me to detest false modesty) going at each other hammer and tongs, tongues, nipples, the glorious space between our legs. Madness. Complete.

"

MICHELLE CLIFF

Crocodilopolis

B Y THE TIME we arrived, at the beginning of September 1905, we had been traveling for one month, give or take a day. We landed at Alexandria, having embarked in Marseilles on the penultimate leg of our journey. From Alexandria we took the train to Cairo and there spent the night under the aegis of the British consul. We had sent ahead letters of introduction, the social instruments necessary for entry.

I do think that one of the only uses of Empire is ease of travel—for us, anyway.

The place was of course terribly hot. My skin seemed to retain the heat so that in bed under the white netting it was as if I radiated. I thought I could see the heat waves in the darkness. Emanations. I longed to perspire, to be bathed in sweat, but I was bone dry, burning. More water, my girl. I got up and walked through the consul's residence and found myself in a walled garden. The street sounds of Cairo were almost nonexistent at that late hour, a few voices raised here and there, a dog barking. I sat on a bench and tried to ignore the heat in my body. After a bit I got up and returned to my room.

In the morning we set sail down the river toward our destination.

On the boat there managed to be something of a breeze, and the heat was tempered by the blue of the waters lapping at us.

At least the blue purveyed a visual coolness.

I don't know what I was thinking. I had on a plaid taffeta dress, which brushed the ground, and a leghorn straw hat, tied under my chin with a ribbon of the same plaid.

I cannot tell you the relief when I gave myself leave to untie the ribbon.

I longed for white linen, loose.

I longed, I must say it—I have been avoiding it, even to myself—for you.

A month had not cooled me.

Photographs of our peripatetic ilk are commonplace. Newsprint, family albums, postcards. "Millie is seated on the ship of the desert," begins the greeting. "Note Sphinx in distance." Millie will sally forth and burn. Oh, my goodness. Not very nice. I confess to an arrogance about the Millies of this world.

Perhaps I should have petitioned Worth. Not much hope there. The man had designed the bell sleeve, after all. Confinement was the order of the day.

I had a desire to remove all my clothes, down to my underthings, venture even beyond that, and sink myself into the dark blue. Even as the man-eaters swarmed on the banks, in the bulrushes. I would open my legs and the Nile would flood me. The man-eaters, their hides as if islands. I'd straddle one and ride him downstream. As queer as Millie on her ship of the desert. For had I not partaken of the most forbidden thing?—short of matricide, that is.

THE SUN RIGHT THEN was heating the boards of the deck and traveling the railing where I stood. I felt the heat in my soles. Passing through my entire body.

In the distance a flock of ibis sat in the naked branches of a tree I did not recognize. Two birds seemed to duel, curved beak against curved beak. Or perhaps that was their mating ritual.

I turned from the river and returned to my cabin and my books.

W E'D HIRED an Egyptian woman to do for us. The consul had recommended her. She was industrious and honest. And clean, the consul's wife stressed. A rarity among these people, she commented, in that ordinary, predictable tone. Were it not for Empire, and its need for caretakers like herself and her hubby, she'd be setting a tea table in St. John's Wood with the help of her Irish maid, whom she would also commend as a rarity among her people. Superiority must be claimed in all things, including one's choice of servants.

T HE EGYPTIAN WOMAN was presented to us. She was swathed in white cotton, almost blue in its coolness. Yes, she said, she was willing to accompany us; she had family near where we were going and she was eager to see them.

On board she trod barefoot on the planks of the deck.

As soon as we reached the site I would free myself of this traveling regalia and dress likewise. I envied her way of moving, so unlike my own, except in dreams, and secrecy. As you know.

She spoke good enough English, which was to our advantage since none of the rest of us was particularly adept at Arabic. My second language was French, and I had studied Greek for ten months with a Miss Threadgill, a friend of the family. Shabby genteel spinster on the face of things. A woman who had come to grief, as the euphemism goes, but not in the usual way. She had spent a stretch of time in Bethlem Royal Hospital, having committed a crime beyond conventional punishment. I was not supposed to know anything about this circumstance.

O UR PARTY WAS four in number. Myself, the Egyptian woman, my brother Vincent, and his friend Hugh Waterman.

"I AM ADVENTURE!" my grandmother, whom I adored, would declaim at table, after a few glasses—Veuve Cliquot Brut—but she was not a woman who depended on wine for her explosions of self.

No, indeed.

As a girl I sat on her four-poster bed and we traveled around the world she had never seen. She was rather like Prester John, imagining creatures in far-off places, at the edge of the world, tumbling off.

Beings with umbrellas growing from their foreheads.

Women with golden nipples, dripping Golden Syrup.

Volcanoes inhabited by fire-people, who burned but were unconsumed. Unlike one of Bosch's infernal landscapes. Here fire was a blessed thing, lighting the chamber inside the volcano. And the unconsumed the opposite of damned. "Life should be made of fire," my grandmother said. "Not immolation but a blaze of light."

SHE DIED FINALLY sliding down a banister. I was in my room one night when I heard a sharp "Ooh!" and then a thud. I ran toward the sounds and found her in her nightdress, in a heap at the foot of the staircase, one thin line of blood at the corner of her mouth. I closed her eyes, now emptied of imagination, and enfolded her in my arms. I sat there until she grew cold. The dawn began streaming through the stained glass windows and lit upon us. One of the servants, on her way to light the fires in the bedrooms, came upon our pietà, gave a cry, and ran off to fetch my brother. That day I moved into her four-poster, where I spent my grief.

THE BOYS—now in their thirties—had met at Oxford. I had been educated at home—in my grandfather's library, my grandmother's four-poster, through the Greek lessons of an apparent madwoman. I followed where my own mind led me, unconfined by curriculum. That's one way to regard it.

It was I who had located Crocodilopolis in the first place. Quite by accident. In the library one evening I found Strabo's *Geography* and decided to practice my Greek.

There it was: Crocodilopolis, Shedet, the separate one, "the oasis that was not an oasis," according to Strabo, "a place of dalliance."

THE CROCODILE EMERGED in silence and in mystery from the waters of Nun, the primeval sea which drained into the Nile. Its back an island, represented earth, its membraned eye, the sun, and it was given life by way of water.

In the crocodile was all creation found.

In Crocodilopolis were his temples and his tombs.

Strabo describes the sacred crocodile, vicar of Sobek, crocodile god. A tamed creature decked in ornaments of glass and gold, its forefeet braceleted and painted, holding court for pilgrims bearing offerings. The creature lived in a lake on temple grounds in a state of divine captivity. It drank milk sweetened with honey and was fed grains and meat. On its death the creature was embalmed by priests as if it were a pharoah. Its mummy was carried through the streets of Crocodilopolis in a sacred procession until it reached the temple where the mummy was placed on an altar, its final resting place.

The internal organs, but for the heart, had been removed. A scarab was placed at the heart, the seat of brilliance.

Inside the mummy was a rumor of language. It was that we sought.

THE TABLE was set in the main cabin. An earthenware vessel of black olives sat at its center. As I was waiting on Hugh and Vincent to arrive I poured myself a glass of red wine from a terracotta pitcher with a curve of blue, the Nile, running down its side. We were to join the captain for the evening meal. There were no other passengers. We had hired the boat to take us downriver to a place called El Wasta, where we would secure overland transportation to deliver us to Crocodilopolis.

The captain came in through the jalousied doors and greeted me. Behind him, through the opened doors, was the river. I listened for the yawns of crocodiles. All I heard were the sounds of the boys' approach.

Hugh's voice, high-pitched one moment, basso the next, as I imagined Oscar Wilde might speak, heralded: "I came upon Isis and Osiris: I had done a deed, they said, which the ibis and the crocodile trembled at. I was buried for a thousand years, in stone coffins, with mummies and sphinxes, in narrow chambers of the heart. I was kissed by crocodiles."

"I think you left a bit out," Vincent said.

"Only by way of improvement, old boy. I don't think DeQuincey would mind, if in his stupor he managed to notice."

"Ah, the importance of being you."

The two entered the room.

"I believe it was 'cancerous crocodiles,' dreadful image, the opium-eater's remorse, I expect." Vincent would not let go.

"Don't be tiresome," Hugh replied, as he cast his gaze across the brownness of the Egyptian woman, who carried a silver platter laden with tomatoes and cucumbers dressed with mint and olive oil and lemon juice, breads dotted with toasted sesame seeds, lamb kebabs spiced with zatar, which she placed in front of us on the dining table. I tried to meet her eyes but was unable.

AFTER DINNER I went for a stroll around the deck. In the dark a half-moon reflected off the waters. And that which I had submerged came up for air.

You turn onto a narrow lane which branches from a secondary road. The lilacs are on the verge, at the edge of a cowpath, worn down over the years, widened by rainfall. It is May in the dream and we are in England. I follow you at a distance.

This is a chance encounter. Is the house still there, are you, visible from the flagstone path? The trace of vegetable garden, the copper beech.

Rosebushes, "heavy feeders," as you once said. "As we are." Fragrant Cloud, deep-red bloom with one dark petal as if bruised. "As we were."

ROSE TREES are numerous in the Fayum—our destination. Most attar of roses of Egypt is manufactured there. The air will be heavy with their scent. Even unbearable.

I dreamed about the date May 5, 1895. We were together in a small room with others, people I did not recognize. I told you about the dream. You said: "That was the day my mother died. And you don't think we are connected. You think this is some romantic adventure, some of the rule-shattering in which you like to engage."

Then: One last letter from one disastrous afternoon:

Yesterday when I chose those flowers I did feel, as I said, they somehow represented us. I think the depth of color, scent. The sweetness of roses, the sharpness of ginger. The strict cultivation of one, the ruinate wildness of the other. How one can have both, be both. As we . . .

That is all I can remember. I burned the letter, along with all the others. Not such a daring girl, after all.

You stop walking and turn and see me. Throw a kiss.

Your bed, still. The room clouded.

What a stunning secret.

Of which I cannot let go.

I woke in the dark of my cabin and ran my hands over my body. I slipped off my nightdress and felt the heat of my skin under the Egyptian cotton sheets.

A place of dalliance.

I knew I could not stay here in this bed, could not sleep. I got up and put on a robe and began to pour a glass of brandy to settle my thoughts, then a light came on outside the door. And I swear I thought I would find you on the other side of the jalousie. I almost convinced myself. I opened the door and saw it was but moonlight. Idiot. I heard the boys' giggles a few doors down. Since there was nothing else I decided to take a stroll. I set out barefooted along the deck and felt the warmth of the boards flooding me again. Again I was drawn to my memories. Wanting now to banish them I stood at the rail and watched the outline of the crocodiles, their island hides riding the surface of the river.

SEVERAL DAYS PASSED. We were nearing our destination. I had hoped the distance, the adventure, would aid forgetting.

Our affair because of its nature had been parabolic. The passion between us, unlike anything I had known (had even imagined was possible, a young lady's imaginings should not venture there, into those dark, wet places), would not die down, did not take what I imagined would be its natural (that word!) course but existed in spurts, followed by bouts of rage, terror. What possible future could we have? Two intelligent, beautiful women (my grandmother taught me to detest false modesty) going at each other hammer and tongs, tongues, nipples, the glorious space between our legs. Madness. Complete. We had in our misbehavior no center of gravity.

"Do you realize they would have burned us at the stake?"

"At the very least, my love."

Forgetting is impossible. Distance holds no comfort because I hold all of it inside of me and am lived in by thoughts of you, us. The physical is one thing, one unimaginable thing, but there is another dimension to all this, which has hold of me and—

And what?

Try to concentrate on what lies ahead, on what might be uncovered, discovered.

"I am Adventure!"

Bewitched. She knew that state. She lived there.

The body remembers what the mind thinks it has forgot. April. A rainy afternoon. Green outside the window. A river behind the woods behind the cottage. The body remembers, becomes wet.

WE SHALL BE landing tomorrow and taking a caravan the remaining distance to Crocodilopolis. It is a journey of four or five days. We will lodge in tents.

Are we so different from other grave robbers? I wonder.

Nonsense. We seek poetry, not pots. The words the Aeolian lyre accompanied. The *disjecta membra* of a queer and brilliant people.

"THE PERFECT LOVE AFFAIR is akin to the perfect murder. Ideally, only two people should know about it."

One of the boys was pronouncing outside my tent. I could not ascertain which one; their speech patterns had become unnervingly similar.

The Egyptian woman very kindly has given me a pair of white trousers and a white shirt. I will use the excuse of ease of movement for my masculine dress in case anyone inquires.

I am reading a book by Amelia B. Edwards, an Englishwoman who fled to Egypt in middle age when her parents' deaths freed her. She writes:

". . . a magnificent fragment containing nearly the whole of the second book of the Iliad . . . the three oldest Homeric texts previously known came from the Land of the Pharoahs. . . . Other papyri found within the century contain fragments of Sappho, Anacreon, Thespis, Pindar, Alcaeus, and Timotheus; and all, without exception, come from graves.

"The great Homer papyrus of 1889 was rolled up as a pillow for the head of its former owner. . . . its former owner was a young and apparently beautiful woman, with little ivory teeth and long, silky black hair. . . . She may have been Egyptian, but she was more probably a Greek. . . . She so loved her Homer. Her Homer is now in the Bodleian. Her skull and her lovely hair are now in the South Kensington Museum."

The dream separated from the dreamer. Ensconced she is today in the Natural History Museum, among the taxidermy. Her favorite poem, companion in the afterlife, the property of scholars, old men, young men, querulous no doubt of the intellect of this apparently beautiful woman, if they are even aware of her.

I am also reading John Addington Symonds on the Greek poets and take heart particularly in his outrage at the destruction of Sappho's poetry. But even in his outrage he cannot accomodate her passionate bent and so changes the pronouns in her hymn to Aphrodite from she to he. As with Swinburne's "Sapphics," which Symonds touts, the eternal scholarly struggle to combine respect and loathing.

The odor of roasting lamb is in the air. The Egyptian woman is preparing the meat on a spit over a bed of coals. The lamb was slaughtered this morning by two of the men who operate this caravan. They took it off a distance so we, with our foreign sensibilities, were spared its cries.

Not so different from England, where our cruelties are left to others and we personally are spared. But I will never become a vegetarian.

Later, after dinner, I strolled into the surrounding oasis and came upon the shallow grave of the slaughtered lamb. Its skin had worked its way to the surface or had been pulled there by some other animal perhaps. I touched its pelt with my bare foot. Soft, silky.

The Egyptian woman is outside my tent, an envelope held in her left hand.

"For you."

"Thank you." I take the envelope from her, hoping against hope, knowing it is from you. It is much traveled, as if you are in my pursuit. How I wish that were so.

The Egyptian woman turns and leaves.

O N THE CAMP STOOL outside the tent I study your hand.

> My heart,
>
> I know not when, if this will reach you. I am sending it via the consulate in Alexandria. Please forgive me for interrupting your adventure. I must write because I am afraid of what may happen to me, over which I have no control. I am afraid . . .

Whence is she writing me? From her bedroom, where she conceals her correspondence in the webbing of a chair that she weaves and reweaves as if Arachne?

I can see her. The straight-backed chair pulled up against her writing table. The gaslight casts a yellow glow on the wallpaper of her room. Primroses, as I recall. The drapes are heavy, velvet. If it is evening they will be drawn. Their greenness shutting out the light and noise of a street in Hampstead. On her mantel over the gasfire is a display of family memorabilia. Long-haired, soft-featured women and sharp, mustached men. A print by Lady Butler, gift of an aunt and uncle, over the mantelpiece. *Calling the Roll After an Engagement, Crimea.* "Into the valley of death . . . valiant six hundred." The legend etched in brass on the frame. Over her bed print of a crofter's cottage, two girls at play in a barnyard, puss sips milk from a blue-willow bowl. On the bedside table are the books she dips into to pass the time.

Our actions trespassed these virginal environs. Shattered them.

"I wish there was a safe place. There is no safe place. Not on your caravan. Not in the middle of the desert. Not in some Egyptian ruins. Safety is found only in the grave. Safety—I crave safety. You were right to call me a coward. Passionate coward, but coward nonetheless. Enslaved by things conventional."

We had not committed the perfect love affair. Her family had found out and were threatening a cure. For me there was no going back. She hoped her case might be different. That they might forgive her and forget. That a dowry would be settled on her, a suitable match arranged. Then the doctors were brought in. She was given milk and zwieback and put to sleep. Ever after: silence.

> The moon has set and the pleiades; it is midnight, and
> time goes by, and I lie alone.
>   —Sappho #168B

AT LONG LAST: "Look," The Egyptian woman says, indicating the horizon. "There."

And there it is.

I am standing in the ruins of the Crocodile god's temple. As promised, the air is heavy with the flesh scent of roses. Their fragrance reigns. On either side of me are pink granite stumps, what remain of pink granite columns. Bits of mica and feldspar in the stone glitter as shafts of sunlight reach them. The temple floor had been paved in pink granite as well. According to accounts by Strabo and Herodotus the doors had been covered with sheets of hammered gold. These are no more. I am almost overcome by the sweetness of the air, by what lies around me. Scattered over the temple floor, a sea of fragments, poetry, and the pink granite becomes the ocean floor.

I sink into the sea of fragments. Alive.

RON MOHRING

The Sound

I'm digging in the garden when I hear it, an inhuman grating,
a wrenching moan and I think it's an injured child and drop
my shovel and step into the street to look, the kind of sound

a dog might make in grief, my neighbor's unloading something
from his truck, the tailgate's open and there's this awful keening
as he carries boxes back and forth, it's the rusted hinges rubbing

but I can't let go of it, the sound the body would make in protest,
and I've slipped from the school bus steps, landed on my back
on the rainy pavement, everything collapses, my body buckling

and unbuckling, trying to force air back into my lungs, I stagger
up the walk like a long blackening tunnel toward the school,
my vision flickering, this horrible sound engulfing me, a human

accident, a body wreck, a wracking shuddering bass, Diana
Winterberger pounding me on the back, screaming *He can't
breathe!* as people swirl around me, I'm parting my classmates

like a messenger with terrible news, and Neal Brandenburg,
the school punk, turns from his locker with a sour *I always said
that kid was queer*, and Mr. Dennison, the coach, is running

toward me as I pivot halfway up the stairs and everything
goes black and the next moment I'm in his downstairs office,
he's leaning over me, I'm listening for that sound and only then

understand it had been coming out of me, his face is close to mine,
I think of his nickname, Peachy, the boys in gym class say he can't
grow a beard, *I'm sorry*, I say, *It's not your fault*, he says, *What*

happened, he says, and I want to ask him what that other boy
was talking about, *I fell off the bus*, what did it mean, *I hit my back*,
and he helps me sit up and asks if he can lift my shirt to look,

I can't believe his hands could touch me and not hurt, but I nod,
there in the pocket of quiet surrounding us both.

Space Exploration

Silent black and white: the sixth birthday party
of my own mother,
who would not imagine the word *ovary*
for a decade.

A screenful of busty gray women
in a Brooklyn yard.
The moon faces ache with expectation
of blossoming bloodlines, freshly painted
houses, children's children's children—

and the cavern in my center
grows black
as the low-humming danger of stories.

Look at their palms wrinkled
into waves, their air-kisses
just a thin screen away from me,
the one who has chosen
to be childless:
the last of them.

The hum hollows me
into a gourd, dry, implacable: *tick whir*
says the tape, *tell us*
you are a woman,
tell us you are not for nothing,

beg the women. *Tell us
you won't kill us.*
Oh mothers, I say
from the brittle gourd:
I do not want to end you.

The sixth birthday party
of my own mother,
who had no idea.
Sugar crust, fiery cake,
elasticked hat. On her father's knee.
Turn around and look at him
when he talks to you!
Don't you know he'll be dead
in a year?

Turn around and look at him. On her father's knee, my mother
squirms, his breath at her ear. Her mother blows candles with her,
back still strong, family living. The girl's hat loosens and the sugar
melts into her tongue: my mother.

My father's breath at my ear. My father,
forever pushing up horn-rims. My mother,
hair back thick and black. They watch
me perform on little legs, mouth
sweet and small as a grape *Do* something
for the camera! On a tricycle, plunging
through the air as if it weren't there.

My sixth birthday party.
I will not imagine
the word *ovary* for a decade.
I have disappointed no one.
I have not yet chosen
to be the end of us.

STACEY WAITE

On the Occasion of Being Mistaken for a Boy by the Umpire in the Little League Conference Championship

I had learned quickly how to spit through
the jail-like bars of the catcher's mask
so looking back I can't say as I blame the umpire who,
after seeing me spit and punch my glove,
could only draw one conclusion:
"You got your cup on, right, son?"

And almost everyone hears him, and I want
my father to stand up, like he does, and yell,
"What the hell are you looking at, bub!"
or "Bad call, blue!" But instead there's a hush,
and I forget the signs for curve balls, fast balls,
and screw balls, and all I can think about is no balls,

no little ten-year-old balls to match my spit
and mitt-punching. My mother pretends
to clean up orange peels and the boys yell
from the infield, "It's a girl, we got a girl as catcher."
He doesn't know what to say so follows up his "Alrighty"
with a quick "Play ball." But I can't squat now,

I think everyone is looking at my no balls.
They're all watching the girl with no balls.
I'm watching her, too. She knows better
than to cry so spits again. She learns
to live in halves, to, as her father says,
"Save it for the field." She snaps,
"What are you, blind, Ump?" and digs
her plastic spikes into the fresh dirt.

TIFFANY LYNN WONG

Ketchup and French Fries

When I was seven, I wanted to be a priest.
I poked three holes through the top of a white

garbage bag and wore it as my robe. Stray cats
confessed to me their sins about the murder

of mice and moths. The neighborhood kids
attended my mass in anticipation of the ketchup

and French fries I served as the blood and body
of our lord Jesus Christ. On Ash Wednesday,

I took the leftovers from my father's cigar tray
and smudged them on my followers. Baby

dolls were brought to me to be bathed in holy
water from my kiddy-pool and squirt gun.

I forbade eating meat on Fridays during Lent,
and I left fish sticks out for the hungry masses.

Magus

I

All things in miniature to love:
a cupboard's shelves arrayed with Delft,
a green felt settee on feral
feet, the effigies of us:
homunculi who lived in dwarf
décor—rubber skin,
mouths tasting air,
scalps with holes awled in rows
as though for planting, tendrils
sprouting. I combed, curled, sprayed,
shook a doll back and forth
to relish the hiss of curls—lashed

lids blinking, the doll thinking:
What are you doing to me?
I'm a friend of your family,
I thought back.

II

"I'm a friend of your family," a thin
woman announced, meeting me after school.
With bisque skin and eyebrows
penciled into commas, she spoke

little as she drove to her clapboard house
and smuggled me up musty stairs

to an attic realm of dolls—hundreds
fanned out on shelves:

startled, drowsy, dazed in cambric
and onion-colored lace. I fell
asleep beneath their blinking eyes
as beneath a stipple of stars.

Voices tumbled toward me,
umbels of ash dissolving
at the touch of boy flesh, "Wake up,
it's time to go back to your mother."

III

Back home. All things in miniature to love
for the grown things they might become. Father
to adult puppets, and also their child, I
grew them as they grew

into me. Together in our cinder-block
cellar—flanked by angels, clowns, kings—
I sewed and glued costumes,
crowns, wings; scored and daubed

holiday tableaux for my family.
As my hands filled torsos
with vertical life, fire-
red curtains parted into hair.

Like a harvest moon, a giant rose:
my head. Spiraling from vinyl grooves, actors'
voices conjured seasons.
Inside those words both said and sung

—as my hands waltzed inside shadowy
puppet-sleeves—I heard, "Magic
boy, you can grow yourself up,
the night sky blooming cups of flame."

Hummingbird

Legless, you hoist
your jewelled belly
to meet the air.

Stopper of time,
the smoky red perfume
of your thoughts' jubilant
sweetness a cloud of mist;

bliss messenger,
how you hoist your refusal
of the idea of mass,
dissolving into alchemy.

I love your fool's
courage—
that curious dip
in the chasm of ether.

CONTRIBUTORS

CHERYL B. is a writer who has performed her work throughout the U.S. and internationally. Her favorite flower is the violet. Among her favorite queer authors are Audre Lorde and Allen Ginsberg. A native New Yorker, she lives in Brooklyn and online at www.cherylb.com.

RAFAEL CAMPO teaches and practices internal medicine in Boston. Most recent books are *Landscape with Human Figure* (Duke, 2002); and *The Healing Art: A Doctor's Black Bag of Poetry* (Norton, 2003). For more information, please visit www.rafaelcampo.com. Favorite flowers are lilacs, peonies, gardenias, and lilies-of-the-valley; queer writers who have been most influential and inspiring are Reinaldo Arenas, Federico García Lorca, Thom Gunn, Marilyn Hacker, Richard Howard, Audre Lorde, Adrienne Rich, and Walt Whitman.

MARY BETH CASCHETTA'S fiction has appeared in *The Red Rock Review*, *Mississippi Review*, and *Blithe House Quarterly*, among others. *Ms.* magazine called her first collection of stories, *Lucy on the West Coast* (Alyson, 1997), "a spectacular collection of women and girls, fugitives and ghosts, invalids and activists." Recipient of the WK Rose Fellowship, she is currently working on her first novel in Massachusetts, where she lives with her wife (!), Meryl Cohn, also a writer. Her current favorite flower is the petunia, as much for the sound of the word, as for the bloom.

ANGELIQUE CHAMBERS likes Gerber daisies, fiesta ware and other tacky things. She would like to thank Alix Olson, Dorothy Alison, and Minnie Bruce Pratt for teaching her that bad girls with dirty mouths can be poets too. This is her first publication.

A fan of peonies, **CLIFFORD CHASE** is the author of the memoir *The Hurry-Up Song* and the editor of the anthology *Queer 13*. Inspirations for "The Tooth Fairy" include Rebecca Brown's *The Gifts of the Body* (for its rigorous concision) and Wayne Koestenbaum's long poem "Rhapsody" (for its sparkling thought-nuggets).

MICHELLE CLIFF'S novel *Free Enterprise* will be reissued by City Lights Books in September 2004. Her favorite flower is Fragrant Cloud, a deep red rose with one burnt petal. Walt Whitman, Elizabeth Bishop, Pier Paolo Pasolini—she is currently working on a translation of "Gramsci's Ashes."

TIM DOUD is represented by Priska Juschka Fine Art in NYC and MCMagma in Milan, and is currently having a solo show at Galerie Brusberg in Berlin. He teaches at American University in Washington DC. "I've always really admired Paul Cadmus and have an interest in Jared French's work. More contemporary Queer artists, painters, there is Frank Moore, who recently died and David Wojnorowicz (also dead). I also like the work of painter Kurt Lauper from LA." Favorite flower: the pansy.

QWO-LI DRISKILL is a Cherokee Two-Spirit also of African, Irish, Lenape, Lumbee, and Osage ascent. Hir work has been influenced by Chrystos, Colin Kennedy Donovan, Janice Gould, Joy Harjo, Essex Hemphill, June Jordan, billie rain, basil shadid, and Alice Walker. S/he loves lilies-of-the-valley, irises, and daisies. Hir first collection of poetry is forthcoming; find out more at www.dragonflyrising.com.

SUZANNE GARDINIER is the author of the long poem *The New World* (Pittsburgh, 1993) and *A World That Will Hold All the People* (Michigan, 1996), essays on poetry and politics. The poems in this issue are sections from another long poem, in manuscript, called *Dialogue with the Archipelago*. She teaches at Sarah Lawrence, dreams of Walt Whitman, and tends a flourishing jasmine in the apartment she shares with her lover and two children in Manhattan.

DAVID GROFF is the author of *Theory of Devolution* (Illinois, 2002), selected by Mark Doty for the National Poetry Series. He's been influenced lately by James Schuyler and Tony Kushner. His favorite flower is wild.

MARILYN HACKER is the author of eleven books of poems, most recently *Desesperanto*, published by W.W. Norton in 2003, along with *First Cities: Collected Early Poems*, and also of three recent books of translations. She received an Award in Literature from the American Academy of Arts and Letters in 2004. She lives in New York and Paris, and teaches at the City College of New York and the CUNY Graduate Center.

DANIEL HALL is currently Writer in Residence at Amherst College. Some influences will be obvious; the less-than-obvious might include Ben Belitt and William Bronk. Favorite flower: a toss-up between hydrangea and white trillium.

GAIL HANLON'S work has appeared in *Rattle*, *The Iowa Review*, *Best American Poetry 1996*, and other journals. She lives in the Boston area. "Influences? Sappho, Wu Tsao, Rich, Lorde, O'Hara . . ."

REGINALD HARRIS'S poems have appeared in *5 AM*, and *Sou'wester*. Influences include Lorde, Hemphill, and Cavafy. Favorite flower: gardenia cf. Peter Lorre in *The Maltese Falcon*.

CHRISTOPHER HENNESSY'S book, *Outside the Lines: Interviews with Contemporary Gay Poets*, comes out in 2005 (University of Michigan Press). Recent work has appeared in *Ploughshares, American Poetry*

Review, and elsewhere. "I'm a wallflower, but oh to be a sunflower!"—
Chennessy@hotmail.com

HOLLY IGLESIAS recently completed a collection of prose poems about
the 1904 World's Fair entitled *Now You See It*. Her critical study, *Boxing
Inside the Box: Women's Prose Poetry*, is forthcoming from Quale Press
in the fall. Current reading includes David Serlin's *Replaceable You*,
Spencer Reece's *The Clerk's Tale*, and Catherine Reid's *Coyote* (to be
released in October). Favorite flower: lilac.

DEAN KOSTOS is the author of *The Sentence that Ends with a Comma*
and *Celestial Rust*. He co-edited the anthology *Mama's Boy: Gay
Men Write About Their Mothers*. His poems have appeared in *Barrow
Street*, *Boulevard*, *Chelsea*, *Rattapallax*, and elsewhere. The queer
poet he never tires of rereading is Hart Crane. His favorite flower is
the parrot tulip.

E. J. LEVY'S stories have recently appeared in *Paris Review* and *Gettysburg
Review*, and one was named in *Best American Short Stories 2003* as among
the year's notables. Levy recently spent time at Edna St. Vincent Millay's
estate, Steepletop, and considers that flower a current favorite. Influences
include Baldwin, Cheever, Isherwood, and Rich.

TIMOTHY LIU'S most recent book is *Of Thee I Sing* (Georgia, 2004).
After a recent trip to Bled, he considers Sweet William and Timothy to
make the loveliest of wildflowers to ever garnish a dish of grilled gilt.

MARY ANN McFADDEN'S first book, *Eye of the Blackbird*, was chosen by
Chase Twitchell for the Four Way Books Intro Series in 1997. Her
poems have appeared in such magazines as *Kestrel*, *The American Voice*,
and *Southern Poetry Review*. She lives in Mexico. Favorite flower: the
"peace" rose.

RON MOHRING'S first book, *Survivable World*, was the 2003 winner of
the Word Works Washington Prize. He received the 2000 Philip
Roth Residency and the 2001–2003 Stadler Fellowship, both at

Bucknell University, where he teaches literature and creative writing. Favorite flower: the little viola that's also known as heart's ease.

CARL MORSE is the author of the chapbooks *Dive* and *The Curse of the Future Fairy*. Four plays are published by Get a Grip Press (London) under the title, *Fruit of Your Loins*. For a number of years, he was Director of Publications at MOMA. Queer influences: his mum; Amy Lowell; John Milton. Favorite flower: pansy.

LETTA NEELY is a Black dyke who lives in Massachusetts. Much of her time is spent making blueprints to dismantle white supremacy. Favorite flower: the dandelion.

MENDI LEWIS OBADIKE is the author of *Armor and Flesh* (Lotus Press) and the libretto for the opera, *The Sour Thunder* (Bridge Records). For more information, visit www.blacknetart.com. Favorite flower: African violet.

CARL PHILLIPS is author of seven books of poetry, including this year's *The Rest of Love*. James White has been a big influence, and Cavafy a huge one. Favorite flower: evening primrose, though cosmos comes close, in a wind especially.

D. A. POWELL'S most recent book is *Cocktails*. His favorite queer writers are Gertrude Stein, Willa Cather, Tennessee Williams, Amy Lowell, Robert Duncan and Federico Garcia Lorca. His favorite flower is cosmos, because it manages to thrive in the poorest conditions. Generally speaking, he prefers wild species over cultivated.

GRETCHEN PRIMACK is a writer, editor, and teacher who lives in the paradisical Hudson Valley/Catskill region. Recent publishing credits include *The Paris Review*, *The Tampa Review*, and *Open City*. She is deeply moved by the work of Sarah Waters, and her favorite bloom is a fat nodding peony.

JOHN ROWELL is the author of the short story collection *The Music of Your Life* (Simon and Schuster), which was a finalist for the 2004 Ferro-

Grumley Prize. He holds a B.A. from the UNC-Chapel Hill and an M.F.A. from Bennington College, and is the recipient of fellowships from the MacDowell Colony and the Sewanee Writers Conference. Gay authors who have influenced his work: Truman Capote, Carson McCullers, Patrick Dennis, Ronald Firbank, Tennessee Williams. Favorite flower: azalea.

ELAINE SEXTON'S first collection of poems is *Sleuth* (New Issues Press, 2003). Her most recent poems and reviews have appeared or are forthcoming in *Art News*, *American Poetry Review*, *Prairie Schooner*, *River Styx* and the *Women's Review of Books*. "G/L writers who have influenced me? Elizabeth Bishop, Frank O'Hara, and my partner, Robin Becker are the flags of my disposition, to quote the master, Walt Whitman. Favorite flower? The hardy, sumptuous peony."

ROXA SMITH was born and raised in Venezuela. She presently lives and works in New York City. Her paintings have been exhibited nationally in numerous solo and group exhibitions. She recently had a show at George Billis Gallery in New York City. Ms. Smith's work can be viewed online at www.paintingsdirect.com or by contacting the artist at: roxasmith@earthlink.net. "My favorite flowers are orchids and my favorite authors are Jeanette Winterson and David Sedaris."

STACEY WAITE was selected as the winner of 2004 Frank O'Hara Prize in Poetry for her collection *Choke*. Her poems have appeared in *Nimrod*, *The Marlboro Review*, *5 AM*, *West Branch*, and other literary journals. Stacey is partial to orchids mostly because of their being so hard to care for. She has asked for the influence of many poets including Ruth L. Schwartz, Olga Broumas, Richard Tayson, and D. A. Powell.

JOHN WEIR: "I live in the East Village and I teach at Queens College/CUNY, which has the smartest students anywhere and the least chalk. I don't like flowers much. 'Queer' writers I like: Helen Eisenbach is swell, and so is Eileen Myles. Plus, I think John Cheever is pretty queer, whether or not he knows it."

TIFFANY LYNN WONG has recently been published in the *Asian Pacific American Journal*, *Monterey Anthology of Poets*, and *Looking Glass*. She is greatly inspired by and wants to be the girlfriend of poets Jessica Hagedorn and Joan Larkin. Her favorite flower is the daffodil. She is currently an M.F.A. student at the University of California Santa Cruz.

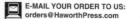

Fall 2004

www.fencebooks.com

SASHA STEENSEN
WINNER OF THE 2004 ALBERTA PRIZE

ISBN 0-9740909-4-8
$12

The poems in Sasha Steensen's splendid A Magic Book offer a feast of paradox—deceptive yet honest, funny but frightening, simple yet mysteriously complex, otherworldy yet wryly quotidian. . . . Wandering the American landscape is her method for moving among materials of our checkered past. . . . Through imaginative exorcism she brings back into our perception the experience of the invisible dead.

SUSAN HOWE

Joyelle McSweeney's *The Commandrine and other Poems* is a necessary series of interrogations. This verse play and poems question what it means to endure knowledge in a global economy. With Yeatsian breadth, McSweeney insists not on anarchy but on an Odyssean journey: beyond the sirens, home. This inventive lassoing-in of reality as we are presently experiencing it leaves no one "clean" or in the clear.   CLAUDIA RANKINE

ISBN 0-9740909-3-X
$12

David S. Allee Kathleen Andersen Ky Anderson Robert
Archambeau Mary Jo Bang Edward Bartok-Baratta Joshua
Beckman John Beer Debbie Benson Walead Beshty Beth Block
Laure-Anne Bosselaar Jenny Boully Joe Brainard Pam Brown
Rafael Campo Jennifer Chang Anna Collette Billy Collins Shanna
Compton Kevin Cooley Michael Costello Jason Danzinger Sarah
Darpli Cort Day Connie Deanovich Albert Flynn DeSilver Geoffrey
Detrani Trane Devore Ray DiPalma Sharon Dolin Brady

ART ESSAYS FICTION PHOTOGRAPHY POETRY

Dollarhide Wei Dong Mary Donnelly Denise Duhamel Richard
Dupont Corwin Ericson George J Farrah MK Fancisco Jay
Gardner Amy Gerstler John Gossage Arielle Greenberg Carl
Gunhouse Jane Hammond Kristen Hanlon Harrison Haynes Lyn
Hejinian Steven A Heller Alexander Heilner Alex Heminway
Stephen Hilger Shannon Holman Henry Israeli Shelley Jackson

C R O W D

Christopher Kelty Lisa Kereszi Barbara Kruger Christine Kuan
Debora Kuan Susan Landers John Latta Brett Fletcher Lauer
David Dodd Lee David Lehman Ben Lerner Luljeta Lleshanaku
Timothy Liu Joyelle McSweeney Richard Meier Lynn Melnick
Charlotte Mew Toni Mirosevich Matthew Monteith Nick Montfort
Malena Morling Paul Muldoon Ryan Murphy Geoffrey G. O'Brien
Kathleen Ossip Ron Padgett Danielle Pafunda Ethan Paquin
Hyun-Doo Park Christa Parravani Chris Prentice Richard Prince

487 UNION ST #3 BROOKLYN NY 11231
WWW.CROWDMAGAZINE.COM

David Prete Kathryn Rantala Julie Reid Andrew Rodgers Andy
Ryan Mark Salerno Maureen Seaton Ravi Shankar Steven
Sherrill Lori Shine Amy Sillman Sean Singer Hugh Steinberg AL
Steiner Virgil Suarez Derek Stroup Cole Swensen James Tate
Matthew Thorburn David Todd Wells Tower Laura Gail Tyler
Michael Vahranwald Kara Walker Clay Weiner Timothy
Westmoreland Susan Wheeler Sam White Marina Wilson Ofer
Wolberger Rebecca Wolff Matthew Zapruder Rachel Zucker

spinning jenny

ISSUE NUMBER 8 ON SALE NOW

BLACK DRESS PRESS

www.blackdresspress.com